LOVED BY
Liam

NEW YORK TIMES AND USA TODAY BESTSELLING AUTHOR
MELANIE MORELAND

BOOK 3

ALSO BY MELANIE MORELAND

Age of Ava (Vested Interest: ABC Corp #4)

Insta-Spark Collection written by M Moreland

It Started with a Kiss

Christmas Sugar

An Instant Connection

An Unexpected Gift

Harvest of Love

Men of Hidden Justice

The Boss

Second-In-Command

Mission Cove

The Summer of Us

Standalones

Into the Storm

Beneath the Scars

Over the Fence

My Image of You (Republishing Soon)

Changing Roles

Happily Ever After Collection

Revved to the Maxx

Heart Strings

Dear Reader,

Thank you for selecting the Vested Interest: ABC Corp series to read. Be sure to sign up for my newsletter for up to date information on new releases, exclusive content and sales.

Before you sign up, add melanie@melaniemoreland.com to your contacts to make sure the email comes right to your inbox!
Always fun - never spam!

My books are available in both paperback and audiobook! I also have signed paperbacks available at my website.

The Perfect Recipe For **LOVE**
xoxo,
Melanie

MORELAND
BOOKS INC.

Edited by
Lisa Hollett—Silently Correcting Your Grammar
Cover design by
Karen Hulseman, Feed Your Dreams Designs
Photo Credit Adobe Stock
Cover content is for illustrative purposes only and any person depicted on the
cover is a model.

DEDICATION

To my beta readers, who insisted that Liam and Paige's story be told through their eyes.

You were right.

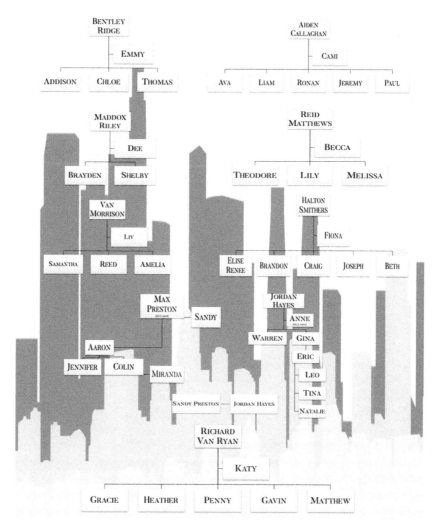

FAMILY TREE

The Contract **VESTED INTEREST**

NEW YORK TIMES AND USA TODAY BESTSELLING AUTHOR

MELANIE MORELAND

CHAPTER ONE
LIAM

The compound was quiet as I reversed my truck out of the driveway and headed toward the gate. I grinned as I spied Pops out on his dock, stepping onto his boat. He loved that thing. I had no doubt he'd putter around on it until Nan would appear, demanding he come have breakfast. I wondered briefly if he'd cajole her into a little trip around the bay. She did love to sail with him.

No one else was around yet, although I knew if I were walking on the beach, I would see Bentley sitting on his deck, sipping coffee, perusing the headlines on his laptop. My dad might be jogging on the beach, intent on keeping strong. If he were, he would head up to join Bentley soon. Even after all these years, the two of them spent an inordinate amount of time together, both in and outside the office.

I passed my brother Ronan's house, the windows dark. I wondered briefly if he was asleep or sitting in the lone chair in his living room, staring out the window over the expanse of water he loved so much, torn up and lost.

I had never seen him so despondent. I couldn't forget the devastated look in his eyes the day I led him away from the corner as he watched the woman he loved walk away.

But hopefully, today, that would change.

"Keep your chin up, little brother," I muttered. "Help is on the way."

I left the compound, a small smile playing on my lips. Ronan had no idea his life was about to get a lot better.

And I, for one, could hardly wait.

I pulled up to the address Ava had given me, studying the small bungalow. Well-kept and tidy, the grass was cut, the bushes trimmed and neat. Some flowers were planted along the front of the house, just beginning to catch and bloom. I looked the yard over with a critical eye, thinking a nice dogwood would look good by the steps and a cedar tree would suit the bare corner.

Then I chuckled. I knew Beth and her roommate Paige rented the house. I was here to pick up Beth and take her to Ronan. Not landscape the place.

I turned into the driveway and cut the engine. Outside, the cool morning air was beginning to warm. I chuckled as I bent and picked up a ball on the grass. It was roughly the size of a soccer ball, but the plastic was various shades of pink. I recalled the many stories Ronan had shared of Paige's daughter, Lucy, and determined the ball must be hers.

Climbing the steps, I admired the two baskets by the door, overflowing with petunias, verbena, geraniums, and ivy. The bright colors added a nice homey touch to the front door and made you feel welcome.

I knocked on the door, and without thinking, bent and dead-headed some petunias while I waited for Beth to answer it. Ava said she would be expecting me.

I was so intent on my task, I was startled when a woman spoke. I hadn't even heard the door open.

"I didn't hire a gardener, so I am going to assume you're not on the clock."

I looked up and froze.

The woman who opened the door was not the one I'd seen with Ronan. It wasn't Beth, so I surmised it was her roommate, Paige.

Jesus, she was lovely.

Straightening, I stared at her openly. She had dark-brown hair that hung past her shoulders in waves and soft blue eyes. She was pretty, with a gentle expression on her face. Her mouth was full, and her smile was warm. She had dimples in her cheeks that deepened when she grinned. The mischievous sparkle in her eyes spoke of humor. I judged her to be about five foot four with pleasing curves I had the craziest impulse to touch. Her gaze was wide, frank, and the way her eyes roamed over me caused my dick to kick to attention in my pants.

I hadn't expected that.

I hadn't expected *her*.

I cleared my throat. "Hey, you must be Paige. I'm Liam, Ronan's brother. I'm here to pick up Beth."

She leaned on the doorframe, crossing her arms. The movement caused her breasts to lift and press together. I was transfixed by the creamy swells. "It's a shame you're already spoken for today. I'd let you pick me up. I bet with those arms you could, too."

I lifted my eyes to hers, and she grinned. She knew I'd been staring at her breasts. They were rather spectacular. The long lashes framing her pretty eyes fluttered, and the slightest bit of color bloomed on her cheeks as our eyes locked.

I wanted to kiss her.

The feeling was so intense, I had to grab the doorframe to stop myself from doing just that.

"Happy to oblige," I uttered, my voice low and raspy. "But I think I need to get Beth to my brother. Perhaps another time."

She bit her lip and stepped back. "Come in. I'll get Beth."

I stepped past her, the scent of her skin hitting me. It was light with various hints of floral notes. As if I were standing in a garden on a summer day, inhaling the sweetness around me.

I wanted to inhale her.

Our gazes locked as I sidled by her, my sheer size making it impossible not to brush up against her. Her tongue darted out, wetting her bottom lip, and it took all I had in me not to cage her against the wall, lower my head, and take that tongue in my mouth.

Somehow, something told me she would let me. She'd open up and allow me to have her full mouth, delve inside and discover the sweetness hiding behind those full lips.

I had to shake my head to clear my thoughts.

I had no idea where they were coming from.

For a moment, we stared. Her breathing kicked up, matching mine. I forced myself not to reach out and touch her.

"Beth?" I managed to get out.

Paige blinked. "I'll get her." She put a hand on my arm, her delicate fingers looking pale and small on my tanned, roughened skin. "She's beside herself, Liam. She's so nervous," she whispered. "I've been so worried about her."

I patted her hand, covering it with mine. "Ronan needs her. I think they need each other."

"I think so too."

A moment passed with me holding her hand to my skin, our eyes locked, a silent conversation flowing between us.

Then she stepped back. "I'll go get her."

"I'll wait here."

She nodded. "Good idea."

She disappeared down the hall, and I leaned against the wall, rubbing my eyes, feeling as if I had just been hit by a Mack truck.

What the hell was that?

Directly below me, I heard voices. I tried not to laugh as I recognized Paige's dulcet tone and heard her words.

"My God, Beth, your ride is here."

Another voice responded. "Okay. Is it Ava or Gracie?"

"It's his brother. The non-triplet one. Heavens, he is enormous. And incredibly sexy." There was a pause. "I want to climb him like a tree."

"Oh, baby, I'd let you," I muttered, straightening my shoulders as I heard them come upstairs. I smiled at the woman I recognized from the office on that terrible day.

"Hi," she said, holding out her hand. "I'm Beth."

I enclosed it in my grip, shaking it firmly. "Hi, Beth. I'm Liam. Ronan's other brother." I winked, looking directly at Paige. "The non-triplet one."

I heard her squeak, and I tried not to laugh. But my smile couldn't be contained.

"Considering I'm a landscape architect, the tree reference was particularly pleasing." My gaze never left Paige's face. "Climbing can be arranged. I'll make sure Beth has my cell number."

Beth glanced over her shoulder. Paige's face was flushed, her eyes locked on me. Once again, her breathing was deeper. Mine matched. It was all I could do not to throw Beth my keys, tell her to drive herself, then grab Paige and drag her down the hall to her bedroom.

The struggle was real.

"Okay, then," Paige responded. "I'll, ah, I'll be leaving now."

She turned and hurried away, and my eyes locked on that rounded, perfect ass. I could imagine the way it would feel, filling my hands.

I looked at Beth, who was watching me with amusement. I lifted one eyebrow in a silent question. "Single, right?" I said quietly.

"Yes." She paused. "With a daughter."

"Lucy," I confirmed. "Ronan thinks she's adorable."

"She is."

"I'll give you my number in the car."

"Okay, then."

"Now—" I grinned "—let's get you to my idiot brother. He has no idea his miserable little existence is about to take an upswing."

"I only agreed to talk to him."

I leaned close, smiling. "I've got a good feeling. And, Beth? I am never wrong."

CHAPTER TWO
LIAM

I chatted with Beth in the car. She was intelligent, funny, and, as Paige had said, nervous. Her hands twisted in her lap so much, finally, I reached over and covered them with mine.

"It's all going to be okay, Beth."

She let out a shaky breath. "You seem so positive."

I glanced at her. "I've never seen my brother so devastated. He knows he fucked up, and he regrets it. Seeing you today will help him." I paused. "You forgiving him would mean the world."

"Let's not get ahead of ourselves," she said, but the words lacked conviction. I had a feeling she was in as much turmoil as Ronan had been.

"So, Paige…" I trailed off.

"What would you like to know?"

"Single, has a daughter—divorced, I assume?"

"Yes. That rat bastard," Beth muttered.

"He hurt her?" I asked.

"He was, is, a narcissistic, arrogant, closed-minded, nasty, worthless piece of trash."

"Tell me how you really feel."

"He didn't treat Paige well anyway, but once he found out about Lucy's partially developed limb? The bastard deserted her. Both of them," she spat. "He deserves nothing but contempt."

"Ronan said she was born with one arm partially formed?"

"Yes." Beth turned in her seat, no longer nervous. "She is the sweetest little girl, Liam. Her smile could light up a room. She's good-natured, never complains, and has adapted so well. There is hardly anything she can't do—and nothing she won't try. She's a pure delight."

"Ronan said as much."

"I can't imagine walking away from my child for any reason. Especially over a missing piece of bone. Still," she sighed. "Paige is better off without him. From what she has said, he wasn't very nice."

"Was it physical?" I asked, tightening my hands on the wheel.

"No. Mental abuse. He belittled her a lot. She hides it, but he did a number on her." She drew in a deep breath. "She's wonderful. A great mom, a fabulous friend, and she is so important to me."

I pulled up to the gate, waiting as it opened.

"I can feel that," I said to her.

"I don't want to see her hurt."

We arrived at Ronan's place, and I turned in my seat, meeting Beth's gaze. "I don't plan on hurting her, Beth. But something hit me when she opened the door. If she's willing, I want to explore it."

"Even with a child involved?"

"That doesn't frighten me. I love kids. It doesn't faze me that Lucy has one arm. I don't care about that. I care about the fact that Paige was hurt. I only hope she'd be willing to give me a chance."

"I think she could be persuaded," she said dryly. "Did you see the way she was eyeing you up?"

I grinned. "Checking out the tree trunk. I caught that." I winked. "Now, enough. Take my number so you have it, and give it to Paige if she asks. I'll take it slow if that's what she needs."

I waited as she typed my number into her phone.

"Come on, I'll take you inside. He's going to be happy to see you."

"I hope so."

I winked. "I know so."

A few hours later, a different Ronan was sitting across from me at the table in the Hub. He still looked tired, but he was happy. At ease. He couldn't take his eyes off Beth, and his hand remained wrapped around hers whenever she was close. I winked at him across the table.

"Good day, little bro?"

"The best." He leaned closer. "Beth says you brought her."

"Yep."

"Thank you."

I squeezed his shoulder. "You owe me."

He grinned, the mischievous look in his eyes back in full force.

"Beth also says you have the hots for Paige."

I met his eyes. "She's right."

"I like her a lot. And Lucy. Don't be messing with them."

I lowered my voice. "Have you ever known me to mess with anyone, Ronan? I felt something for Paige the second she opened the door. She felt it too. I plan on seeing her. Seeing where it goes. Whatever speed she sets is fine with me. And I look forward to meeting Lucy." I waved my finger between us. "So, we good?"

He pursed his lips. "I'll be watching."

I sat back, picking up my mug. "Watch away, little bro. You may learn a thing or two."

He chuckled. "Okay, then."

I swallowed the last of my coffee. "Just so we're clear."

Tuesday afternoon, my phone rang. I pulled it from my pocket and answered.

"Hey, Ronan."

"Bro, I am about to repay your kindness from Sunday."

"Is that a fact?" I asked dryly. "How so?"

"Tacos. At the house with Beth, Paige, and the kids, as well as Paul and Jeremy. Tonight. I'm picking up all the stuff. We're making them a feast."

I was down with that. I loved tacos—my whole family did. My brothers and I made awesome tacos and often whipped them up for the family.

"Are you sure?"

"Paige asked if you were coming when I called to make sure it was okay."

That information made me smile.

"What can I bring?"

"Stop by Paso's and get some fresh tortillas."

"Salsa, guac, and chips too?"

"Of course."

"How about some wine for the girls?"

"They'd like that."

"What about the kids?"

"They love chocolate milk. I know it's always a treat for them."

"Done. What time?"

"Six."

"I'll be there."

He chuckled. "I knew you would be."

I arrived bearing bags of fresh tortillas, plus the extras I had suggested, the packages heavy with containers of salsa and guacamole. I put them in the neat kitchen, grinning at the piles of ingredients Ronan had brought, then joined my brothers on the floor to build Lego stuff with Evan. He was a shy kid, small for his age, but he was intelligent and smart, and after a while, he lost some of his shyness, his smile reminding me of Beth's.

I was drawn to Paige, my gaze falling on her over and again. She met my stares with her own frank appraisals, and my body warmed to her ogling. Something passed between us every time our eyes locked, and more than once, I had the urge to find an excuse to get her alone in another room. My fingers longed to touch her, and I wanted to feel her mouth underneath mine. But what stopped me was the little girl perched on her mother's knee.

Lucy was a walking sunbeam. She stared at all of us "giants" in wonder, her grip on the little teddy in her hand tight. She looked like Paige other than her eyes which, strangely enough, reminded me of my own. She was tiny and sweet, and I could see how much she wanted to join us, but I figured the sheer size of the bunch of us was holding her back.

I pretended to fumble with a couple of pieces and met Lucy's gaze. "I need help, Lucy. My hands are too big."

She hesitated, then slid from her mother's lap and came over to me. I couldn't hold back my smile as she took the pieces I offered and snapped them together, then handed them back.

"Good job, Munchkin," I praised, noting how she used the partial limb to hold the pieces in place. "Maybe you want to help me some more?"

She pursed her lips, then nodded. "Otay."

I lifted her over my shoulder, setting her on my lap. "Okay."

She regarded me seriously. "You hafta hold Mr. Teddy."

"I can do that."

"He only has one arm like me."

"That makes him extra special."

She scrunched up her nose, looking adorable. "Yeah?"

"Yep. And do you know what I brought for an extra-special little girl?"

"What?"

I leaned down, keeping my voice low. "Chocolate milk."

Her eyes widened and her smile broke out. I swear the sun had nothing on this little angel's smile. I wanted to bask in the warmth of it.

Grinning, I handed her another pair of bricks, watching as she looked them over, then snapped them together. I met Paige's eyes, the quiet hope and happiness reflected in her gaze. I nodded slightly, and she smiled, dropping her eyes to her glass. She knew what I was telling her without words.

I was serious about this.

Later, as my brothers and I chopped and prepped, nudging one another out of the way, laughing and teasing, I grabbed the bottle of wine to refill the girls' glasses. I swooped Lucy off the counter onto my shoulder, grinning at the way she clutched my hair for balance.

I caught the tail end of a sentence as I walked into the living room.

"He is one hell of a man," Paige hummed.

I couldn't stop my grin as I filled their glasses. I noticed Paige's flushed cheeks and glanced up at Lucy with a wink, teasing, "I think your momma was talking about me again."

Paige tossed her hair, the light shimmering on the dark strands. "I don't think so."

I laughed, knowing I was correct. Beth and Paige as well as the kids had been invited to brunch on the weekend by my parents. "So, Sunday, I'll be here about nine. We can have coffee before we head out."

"I don't recall inviting you," she retorted, a smile playing on her lips.

I turned and walked away, making sure to hold tight to Lucy. "You were planning on it. I was just saving you the trouble." I disappeared into the kitchen, and I heard her huff.

"Incorrigible," she muttered.

She hadn't seen anything yet.

It appeared that Lucy decided I was okay. Maybe even more than okay. She barely left my side, wanting to sit next to me at dinner, and finally slid onto my lap. I pulled her plate beside mine and made sure she got enough to eat. I rolled her tacos extra tight so she could easily eat them with one hand. She liked it when I called her Munchkin, her nose wrinkling in delight. Paige watched us, her gaze alternately amused, worried, and downright anxious. Given the little I knew of her history, I assumed her worry had a lot to do with her ex. I would have to prove to her I was nothing like him. It shocked me a little how imperative that was already, but it didn't cross my mind to try to pull back.

Somewhere, somehow, I knew how important these two ladies were going to be in my life.

CHAPTER THREE
LIAM

Thursday afternoon, I finished a meeting with a potential client. He wanted all the existing gardens and lawns torn up and a completely new design for a set of buildings he had purchased. The gardens were overgrown and choking themselves. He wanted large pathways, with plants that encouraged bees and other insects important to the ecosystem, yet still appealing to the eye. I had sketched out a few ideas and planned to head to my office in Port Albany and draw out more detailed drawings. Mr. Simpson had been enthusiastic, as had his wife, who it seemed would be the one making the final decision. I could see their vision clearly and had lots of ideas on how to make it come to life.

As I drove toward the highway, I realized how close I was to Paige's house. I glanced at the clock, seeing it was almost noon. I knew she worked from home, and on a whim, I swung by one of my favorite deli places and grabbed some sandwiches with chips and cans of cold soda.

I pulled up in front of her house, climbed the steps, and waited patiently after knocking. I could hear her moving around, and she opened the door, a surprised look on her face when she saw me. She was in a pair of dark pants with a pretty blouse in blues and greens that set off her eyes. Her hair was swept up off her face, and she wore a headset attached to one ear.

"Liam," she said, her eyes glancing around in confusion. "Ronan isn't here."

"Good." I held up the bag. "I brought lunch. I thought you might be hungry."

"You brought *me* lunch?" she asked slowly as if she wasn't used to having something thoughtful done for her.

I would have to change that.

"I did. If you let me inside, I'll give it to you."

The playful glint I liked so much flickered in her eyes, and her mouth curled into a teasing grin.

"Are you still talking about lunch?"

I threw back my head in laughter. "Depends. Play your cards right..." I trailed off, leaning close and brushing my lips across her cheek. "You never know."

She giggled, the sound light and happy. Stepping back, she waved her arm. "By all means, come in."

I stepped past her, my size once again making it impossible not to brush against her, especially since I wasn't trying to avoid the contact. I heard her swift inhale of air and felt the way her body shivered. Our eyes locked as I went by, her widened stare filled with awareness. The same way my body felt her warmth and reacted to it.

"I'm right there with you, baby," I thought. "Give us some time."

"I just have to go sign out for my lunch break. I'll be right there." She indicated the kitchen. "Make yourself comfortable."

I set down the bag and placed the sandwiches on the table, adding the chips and sodas. When she joined me, I waved at the pile I had made in the center of the table, looking like an impromptu picnic.

"I didn't know what you liked. I got egg salad, corned beef, and turkey."

"That's great."

I grinned as she went to the refrigerator and came back with a large jar of pickles.

"I love pickles."

She winked. "Me too."

"You gonna turn everything I say into some sort of innuendo?"

She lifted her eyebrows in silent response as she took a bite of the egg salad. I opened the chips and dumped them on the waxed paper the sandwiches were piled on. Paige picked up a curled chip, holding it like a prize.

"Wish chip," she crowed and gobbled it up, the crunch of the fried potato loud.

I chuckled. "Munchkin at day care?"

"Yes. She loves it there. All the kids and toys."

I chewed and swallowed. "She's ah, pretty remarkable."

"I think so."

"I think her mother is as well."

Her sandwich froze midair, and she regarded me warily. "You-you do?"

"Yeah, I do."

"Oh," was all she said.

"I like her spunkiness. She's adorable and sweet. Well-behaved yet mischievous."

"Are you referring to my daughter or me?"

I laughed again. "Both. I think a lot of that comes down to her mother."

She smiled. "Beth says we're two peas in a pod."

"She's right."

We ate in companionable silence, sharing the sandwiches and chips. I drank my soda, but I noticed she didn't. I picked up another curled chip and offered it to her.

"Another wish, Paige?"

She took it. "Best way to end a lunch."

"Not quite the end," I said, pulling two large cookies from a smaller bag, and she chuckled.

"You thought of everything."

"Except coffee."

"That's easy." She stood, switching on the coffee machine. I ogled her openly, watching the way her pants clung to her ass as she moved. The small sliver of skin that appeared over her waistband as she stretched up to get the mugs. She grumbled under her breath, and I stood and reached over her easily, grabbing the mugs. "Got them," I assured her.

Her back pressed into my chest, molding to me. I heard the hitch in her breath and felt her stiffen slightly.

"You should get a little stool. Or keep them on the lower shelf," I observed.

She shook her head, turning her face to meet my eyes. "So few cupboards. I need the lower ones for plates and glasses that Evan can reach."

"I'll make you a stool, then. A safe one."

"Okay."

It took all I had to pull back and not turn her in my arms and kiss her. I wanted to, though. More than my next breath.

I forced myself to sit down, crumpling up the paper and shoving it into the bag. A steaming cup of coffee appeared before me, and the small jug of cream was set down beside it. I offered her a cookie, noting she chose the oatmeal raisin one. I took the chocolate chip, and we both munched quietly for a moment. Then she spoke.

She set the cookie down, wiping her fingers. "Liam, I'm a pretty honest person, so I'm going to lay it on the line here, okay?"

"Perfect. I'm a straight shooter myself."

"I like you. I mean, you're easy to like. So is Ronan. Paul and Jeremy have that ability too."

I grimaced. "I really don't want to be compared on the same scale as my brothers."

She blew out a long breath, frustrated. "That didn't come out right. Your family is very affable. But I like you—specifically. And that is dangerous."

"For whom?"

"Me."

"I like you right back, Paige. More than like you."

"But it's not just me. I have to put Lucy first."

"I understand that. I wouldn't have it any other way."

"Why did you come here?" Her question was forward and direct, so I responded in the same manner.

"Because I wanted to see you. Without my brothers or Beth or anyone else around. Just you."

She smiled sadly. "That would be rare with Lucy. She's with me all the time."

"No, you misunderstand. I know Lucy is your number one. I respect that. Admire it. I have no problem with the three of us together. I just wanted a little time with you to discuss it. To see if it was a possibility you wanted to explore." I paused. "To see if you felt this crazy attraction as hard as I did."

I waited for her answer, my heart beating fast.

"I do," she whispered.

"Why do I sense a but?"

"It's complicated. We're complicated."

"Because you have a child with special requirements?"

She leaned her elbows on the table. "Because my ex was an asshole and destroyed me. Because my daughter is vulnerable. Because I'm a single mom who struggles to make ends meet. If it weren't for Beth living with us, I have no idea what I would do. How I would cope. I know who your family is, Liam. I can't compete with that."

"I don't recall asking you to." I shook my head. "I think I understand Ronan's reluctance to tell Beth about our family a little more now." I reached across the table and covered her hands with mine, startled at how cool her palms were. I rubbed her skin to warm it. "My family and their wealth have nothing to do with me, Paige. I'm my own person, making my own way. I own a landscaping company. I dig dirt and plant trees. I plan gardens and landscapes. It's not a glamorous life. And my family are just people. My mom put herself through school. So did my dad. The only rich one of the bunch was Bentley." I laughed. "His wife Emmy didn't want to date him because of his wealth. He convinced her to look past it to see him. And she did. Tell me, did my brothers come across as entitled pricks the other night?"

"No."

"We weren't raised that way. My family is down-to-earth. They won't look down on you."

"Beth said they were very nice when she met them. Loud but nice."

I laughed. My family were all loud.

"I'll be honest. I'm comfortable. More than comfortable. I own my house because of my parents. They gave those who wanted it a piece of land. We had to pay for the house. We pay our share of taxes. Upkeep. It's our responsibility. My company does really well, but I work hard making it successful."

"That's good?" she asked, seemingly puzzled at my words.

"The point is, it doesn't matter. I don't care if you have lots of money or none, aside from the fact that I don't like to think of you struggling. Would you like me better if I were poorer?"

"No, but the playing field might be more equal."

"I would say our fields are equal. I have more money, you have Lucy. And you're beautiful."

"Stop it."

"You are." I squeezed her hands. "Be honest, Paige. Are you interested? God knows I am. I feel like a raging inferno every time I'm close to you."

"We'd have to take it slow."

I shook my head. "I don't think that's possible with you. I'm not like my brothers. I see something I want, I go for it. I always have done so. I make up my mind, and that is that."

"And you've made up your mind to what—bed me?"

"Nope. Win your heart. Make you and Lucy mine."

"You can't say that. You barely know me. This is the first time we've been alone together!"

"And look at everything we've accomplished. We've set aside the family issue, I've laid my cards on the table, you've agreed to date me, and soon, we'll seal it with a kiss, and I'll be on my way. I'd say a job well done."

She tossed her hair and spoke with a haughty tone that was completely made-up. "I never agreed."

"You didn't say no either. I'm taking it as a win."

"Dating—"

I cut her off. "You look after Evan so Ronan and Beth can spend some time together. They'll do the same for you. I can hang here sometimes. You, me, and Lucy can do things together." I met her eyes and made sure she knew I was serious. "I won't ask you to choose between us. I know Lucy is first. I'm good with that."

"Where did you come from, Liam?"

I winked. "Your wish chips." I waited a moment then asked her, "Well?"

"I want to."

"It makes you nervous."

"I kid around and say outrageous things, but yes, it does."

"Try, baby. Try it with me."

Her response was barely a whisper. "Yes."

I stood and rounded the table, kneeling by her chair. Up close, I could see the worry in her eyes, a worry I wanted to erase. Slowly, I eased my hand around her neck, stroking at the pulse jumping at the base of it. "Now about that kiss."

She clutched at my wrist, her fingers pale and tiny on the thick muscle. She nodded, her breathing suddenly fast as I leaned up and brushed her mouth with mine. Gently, our lips moved together, learning, moving. She slid her hand up my arm, anchoring it on the back of my neck. I slipped my arm around her waist, tugging her closer. I kissed her harder, flicking my tongue over her bottom lip, groaning when she opened for me.

The desire I'd felt for her exploded as our tongues slid together. It was all I could do not to lower her to the floor and explore all of her. I groaned low in my throat as she slipped her other arm around my neck, molding herself to me. I rose to my feet and sat down in her chair, setting her on my lap. Her hands were everywhere, running up and down my arms, her fingers drifting over the expanse of my shoulders, running over my back. She tugged on my hair, burying her hand in the back of it, holding my head close to hers. I stroked up and down her spine, feeling the ridges and bones under my fingertips. I slid one hand under her ass, rubbing it while I cupped the back of her neck, using my fingers to swirl soothing passes on her skin.

I poured everything I had into that kiss. Our first one. I wanted her to feel the yearning I had for her. To know I wasn't kidding when I said I'd never reacted to someone the way I had to her.

Then a timer went off, making her stiffen and pull away.

"My break," she gasped as I trailed my mouth down her neck, pushing aside the edge of her blouse. "I have to get back to work."

"Okay," I murmured, kissing the base of her neck.

"Now, Liam. I have to go now."

"All right." I swirled my tongue on her skin.

"I'll be late."

"Can't have that," I agreed. "You should go." I tugged her earlobe between my teeth, then nuzzled behind her ear.

She whimpered and pulled my mouth back to hers. I kissed her again, groaning at her taste, loving how she felt in my arms. Then I stood and carried her to the little desk where she worked, settling her in the chair and pulling my mouth away. I kissed the end of her nose and handed her the headset she had removed earlier.

"Stop seducing me, woman. Jeesh. You have my number, right?"

"Yes."

"Use it. Call me later. If you need anything, call me sooner."

I dropped a kiss to her forehead. "I'll see you soon, baby. Thanks for trusting me."

I glanced over my shoulder as I headed to the front door. I didn't trust myself to stay. I knew I wouldn't be able to resist her. She was watching me, her lips swollen from mine, her hair messed up from my hands.

Gorgeous.

I adjusted myself in the truck, already planning on our first date. My little brother owed me a favor. I planned on collecting.

Soon.

CHAPTER FOUR

LIAM

Saturday morning, Ronan walked up the steps to my deck, a torn piece of paper in hand.

"Hey," I greeted him. "Coffee is ready if you want."

"Great."

He disappeared inside and came back out with a steaming mug. He sat down and took a long sip in appreciation.

"What's that? A map to buried treasure?" I asked, indicating the paper he had in his hand.

"A flyer I saw when I was at Beth's." He handed the advertisement to me. "It's a little local carnival in her neighborhood today."

"God, we used to love those. The rides and the cotton candy." I chuckled. "Pretty shitty when I think back, but as kids, they were fun."

"Beth has to work, but I was going to take Evan. Ask Lucy and Paige to join us." He glanced at me, a grin on his lips. "You want in?"

"As if you have to ask. I have a job this morning, but I can meet you there. You think Evan can handle the terrain with his crutches? All the cables and shit?"

"If we go slow and help him, I think he could. We'd both be there to assist him." Ronan scratched his head. "I don't think they get to do much stuff like this. Money and all."

"Yeah, I know. The kids would love it. I wonder if they still have that teacup ride thing. Lucy would have a blast." I met Ronan's eyes. "I bet we could win some seriously huge stuffed thing for her. We know all the pitfalls of those games."

He laughed. "Yeah, we do." I had a friend who used to work in one of the traveling fairs in the summer. He gave us some great pointers which we could use today.

"I was going to take them all to lunch at the diner, then head to the fair. You want to meet us for lunch?"

"Around noon?"

"That works."

"Okay, sounds good. Listen, you have plans for Monday?"

He shook his head. "Beth doesn't have study group, so I planned on hanging with her and Evan. Why?"

"Can you add Lucy to that?" I cleared my throat. "I'd like to take Paige on a date. She'll agree if Lucy is looked after by you and Beth."

"Not an issue. I love that little girl. Anytime."

29

"Great."

"So—"

I held up my hand. "No questions yet, Ronan. I don't have the answers. I want to take her on a date. Spoil her a little. I think both the girls, and the kids, need a little of that. Today can be about the kids. Monday will be about Paige. You can pick a night, and I'll make sure Evan's covered. Deal?"

He pursed his lips. "You sound pretty serious, considering it's been, like, a *week*," he pointed out.

I shrugged. "How fast did you fall for Beth? I mean, let's be honest. You were besotted right away."

He chuckled. "You're right. I was. They're pretty hard to resist."

"Yep."

He grinned, his smile the replica of our mother's. Wide and bright. Dad always called us his sunbeams when we were kids. To this day, he called our mother his "Sunshine."

Ronan stood. "Okay, see you at the diner at twelve. Will I tell Paige you're coming?"

I shook my head. "I'll surprise her."

He laughed as he headed down the steps. "Okay, bro. Later."

I watched him stroll toward his house, thinking how much happier he was. Beth was good for him. He was good for her. They made a great couple, and I looked forward to getting to know her better.

Invariably, my thoughts turned to Paige. She'd been on my mind a lot since our lunch. Our talk. Our first kiss. I replayed the moments of having her in my arms over in my mind. She fit there as if that was where she belonged. Her mouth underneath mine had been responsive and sweet. So bloody sweet. She made me laugh with her witty comebacks and smart remarks. I wanted to know everything about her. Her admission that the thought of us dating made her nervous was something I would have to overcome. I would prove to her I was serious—that she wasn't simply a passing thing for me. None of us Callaghans was built that way. When we loved, we loved completely.

And I had a feeling I was already half in love with Paige Winters. And her little angel of a daughter.

If that made her nervous, then it was a challenge I would have to surmount.

I grinned as I stood and went inside to get my keys and head to the jobsite.

I did love me a challenge.

The look on Paige's face when I walked into the diner later was priceless. Her eyes widened, and a smile broke out on her face as I strode toward the table. Beth was talking to them, her pad out to get their orders as I slid into the booth, dropping a kiss to Lucy's cheek and squeezing Paige's shoulder. I caught the tail end of what Ronan was saying, and I nodded. "Yep. Order whatever you want—milkshakes included. I already know what I'm having."

I sat back, letting my arm rest on the back of the booth, my fingers touching Paige. "After, we'll go to the park," I announced. "There's a little fair at the one not far from your place."

Lucy and Evan became excited, both talking at once. Then Evan frowned and shook his head. "I don't know if I can."

I shook my head as Ronan patted him on the shoulder. "It's good, bud. We've got it covered."

He perked up, his grin wide and relieved. "Really?"

"Yep. So let's eat lunch and head to the fair."

Lucy bent over the place mat she had, coloring it carefully, using her prosthetic arm to hold the paper in place as she filled it in with bright colors. I felt the touch of Paige's fingers on my hand, and I glanced up, meeting her lovely blue eyes.

"Thank you," she mouthed.

I winked and flipped my hand, squeezing her fingers. I liked seeing her happy. Seeing the kids happy. I wished Beth could join us, but I decided I would stay and keep Evan busy later so Ronan and Beth had some time to themselves.

Our food arrived, along with the icy cold milk shakes—vanilla all around, except for Lucy, who liked strawberry.

"It's pink," she informed me. Pink, it appeared, always won out when a decision was to be made on anything. It explained her room, socks, T-shirt, and hair things she wore today. I was sure if the coveralls Paige had her in came in pink instead of denim, that would be her choice as well. She was adorable, sipping her shake, taking little bites of the chicken strips she ordered, constantly asking for more ketchup for her fries. I was pretty certain she ate more ketchup than actual food, but I managed to persuade her to eat a little.

She and Evan had a great relationship—that of real siblings. He teased her, yet was watchful, making sure she was okay. She adored him—it was evident in the way she hung on his every word and looked to him constantly for his advice.

A sudden image of the two of them playing on the beach while Ronan and I watched over them hit me. Our houses were close together, so they would see each other all the time, even if they were no longer living together. I had to mentally shake my head. Where that thought had come from, I had no idea, but it was there, and I felt it with a certainty I couldn't dislodge.

"What's wrong?"

I blinked and looked at Paige, who was gazing at me with concerned eyes.

"You stopped eating."

I grinned and winked. "Nothing, baby. Nothing is wrong." I smiled reassuringly. "In fact, everything is great. Really great."

Lucy looked at me, her little brows drawn down. "Momma not a baby."

I chuckled. "It's a fun name. Like I call you Munchkin sometimes."

She shook her head as if I were crazy, making me laugh.

Ronan clapped his hands. "Okay, who is ready for the fair?"

The kids both clapped, and I grabbed the bill. "Let's go, then! Rides await!"

Evan hesitated as he looked around. "There's a lot of wires and stuff."

"We're gonna go slow. Really slow. Once you get past the first part, the ground is pretty even. Liam and I are going to be right beside you. No one will run into you, and if you get tired, we can help. You want to try?" Ronan encouraged him.

Evan squared his shoulders. "Yes."

I grinned. He was a brave kid. Stronger than he looked. Determined. I knew Ronan was looking forward to Dad meeting him. We were both certain he could help Evan.

I bent and scooped Lucy to my shoulders. "Hold tight, Munchkin."

Three hours later, it was a weary group heading back to the cars. Lucy was half asleep, her head resting on my shoulder, too tired to even try to sit on one. Evan was walking slower than he had all day, but his face was wreathed in smiles. Paige carried a massive unicorn with pink feet I had won for Lucy, and Ronan had a smaller elephant shoved under his free arm. Every ride possible had been ridden. Cotton candy, fried donuts, and iced lemonade had been sampled. A wildly colored freehand painting that Lucy had wanted to try making was in a bag. The splatters contained a great deal of pink, although purple, white, and yellow were added to the mix.

I met Paige's eyes. "Will she stay awake until bedtime?"

She rubbed Lucy's back affectionately. "I'll let her sleep for a bit. She can stay up later tonight."

"I'm going to pick up Beth. You wanna come with me, Evan, or you wanna head home?" Ronan asked as I carefully strapped Lucy into the car seat, grateful that it had been one of the standard options on the truck. I had never even looked at it until today.

"I'll go home, Ronan. I'm kinda tired. But it was, like, the best day ever!" he exclaimed.

I helped him up into the cab, noting how he favored the leg. We'd skirted a lot of wires, slowly trod over covered-up cables, and stuck to the edges of the crowds, but he had done it. I could see he was tired and the long afternoon had taken a lot out of him, but his eyes shone with happiness.

"You go get Beth. I'll get this lot home," I said with a grin. Even Paige looked ready for a nap. I wondered how she'd feel about letting me lie down with her, snuggle her close to my chest, and sleep a while. Maybe I'd ask.

With a wave, Ronan left, and I loaded the last of the stuff into the back, squishing the unicorn in last. It was so big, Lucy could ride the thing. The guy manning the throwing booth wasn't happy when I aced the balls in the buckets and won it. His smile was fake when he handed it to me, but I didn't care. Munchkin was so excited, I thought she'd squeeze my neck until I stopped breathing.

I climbed in the driver's seat and held back my laughter. Evan and Lucy were both asleep already. Paige was halfway there. Her eyes fluttered open, and she smiled.

"Thank you," she murmured, her eyes drifting shut again.

I stroked my fingers down her cheek, the skin warm from the afternoon sun. "You're welcome," I replied.

It's only the beginning, I added silently.

Only the beginning.

The fair was only about five minutes from Paige's house, but I drove around slowly for about twenty minutes to let her have a nap. I was certain those were a rare treat for her. I parked in the driveway, leaving the engine running. I quietly opened the back door, Evan lifting his head and yawning.

"We're home?" he asked.

I put my finger on my lips, motioning between Paige and Lucy. He grinned in understanding and slid from the seat, going ahead of me as I carried Lucy into the house. I followed him to her bedroom and laid her on the bed, making sure Mr. Teddy was beside her.

"You should take off her shoes," Evan whispered.

I tugged them off and lifted a light blanket over her.

In the hall, Evan smiled. "I'm gonna go to my room for a bit. Thanks, Liam, for today. It was great."

"No problem. I had fun."

He tilted his head. "You're like Ronan, aren't you?" he said. "A really good guy."

"Thanks, Evan. I try to be."

"You are," he said emphatically, then turned and limped into his room. I heard his bed squeak as he sat down on the mattress, and when I peeked in, I saw he was already deep into building something with his Lego bricks.

I returned to the truck and shut off the engine, smiling at the fact that Paige didn't move. I opened her door, undid her seat belt, and slid my hands under her. She stirred as I climbed the steps.

"What—wait, what are you doing?" she asked, gripping my shoulders.

I set her on the kitchen counter, brushing her hair off her cheek. "You were sleeping. I was hoping to get you into the house and tuck you in. Let you rest."

"Where's Lucy?"

"I got her in bed and took off her shoes. Evan's deep in Lego land."

She yawned, looking rumpled, sleepy, and beyond adorable. Exactly the way I had imagined her waking up beside me in the morning.

"You didn't have to do that, Liam."

I wrapped my arms around her, holding her close. She burrowed into me, feeling soft and small. I liked how she pushed as close as possible, her arms going around my waist, her head resting on my chest.

"I wanted you to have a little rest."

She hummed against my sternum.

"How about I tuck you in bed?"

She tilted her head back, gazing up at me, her eyes warm. "How about we take advantage of the kids being occupied and the fact that we're alone?" she whispered.

I didn't need another invitation. I dropped my head, capturing her mouth with mine. She tasted of candy floss and cinnamon. The kiss started off as a gentle press of our lips, a coming back together of this new, warm feeling of intimacy, then it changed. It became deeper, stronger, and needier. Desire kicked in for both of us, and Paige's arms tightened around me, a low sound escaping her mouth as my tongue delved and swirled around hers. I stepped between her legs, yanking her tight to my torso, feeling the way she molded to me. Her hard nipples pressed against the material of her T-shirt and into my skin. Her fingers played restlessly on my back. She wrapped her legs around my waist, bringing her core flush to my body. With a low growl, I tightened my embrace, tilting her head for better access, and sealed my mouth over hers again. I cupped her ass, encouraging her subtle movements. Drank in the taste and feel of her, desperately trying to maintain some sort of control over myself, knowing the kids were down the hall and this could go nowhere, yet not wanting to stop.

Until the sound of a throat clearing and Ronan's voice startled us apart. "Hey, what's up?"

I glowered at him standing in the doorway, wearing a shit-eating grin. Beth stood next to him, looking shocked.

"Not much, thanks to you."

Paige flushed and slid off the counter. "I have to go and check on Lucy." She hurried away, and I watched her go, frowning. I glared at Ronan for embarrassing her. Beth eased away from him, murmuring about going to see Evan. We were alone in the kitchen, and I crossed my arms.

"What?"

He stepped closer, suddenly serious. "She's a single mom, Liam. That's sacred shit."

"I'm aware."

"I care about her a lot. She's Beth's best friend. Not to mention Lucy and her feelings. You don't trifle with that."

I felt anger roll through me. *"I'm not.* I already told you, I care about both of them. A lot."

He met my gaze, my focus steady and determined. His eyes grew round. "Wow. You're falling for her."

I lost my aggression and stepped back, shaking my head. "Yeah, I am. Both of them."

"You might want to tone down the kitchen groping. The kids like to wander around at times."

I chuckled low in my throat. "Evan is deep in Lego, and the hall floor squeaks. Lucy was in her room, and I could hear her singing away when she woke up from her nap. I knew where they were."

"You didn't hear us."

"I can't listen for everything, Ronan. I thought you were taking Beth to your condo."

He shook my head. "She's exhausted. She needs a quiet night at home, not alone with me at my place. Not sure I could resist her there."

I nodded. "How about pizza for everyone, and we'll go? We can hang together tonight, and we'll be back in the morning to pick them up."

"You going to introduce Paige and Lucy as yours tomorrow?"

My eyebrows shot up in surprise. "I think I need to check with Paige first. We're still figuring things out."

"With your tongues?" he asked mildly, grinning.

I grabbed him in a headlock, laughing.

"Shut up, little brother, or I'll tell Beth about the time you pissed your pants in the woods when you thought you saw a bear."

He grunted as he tried to escape. "I was five, for God's sake. You told me it was a bear that ate bad kids—I was scared for my life!"

Beth and Paige walked in, seeing our wrestling and hearing our conversation.

"Well, this I gotta hear," Paige said with a grin.

I released Ronan with a smirk. "Happy to fill you in."

Ronan groaned, and Beth slipped her arm around his waist, laughing.

"Can't wait to hear it either."

I grinned. He'd think twice about interrupting me again.

CHAPTER FIVE
PAIGE

I stepped from the shower, wiping the condensation off the mirror. I studied my face as I brushed my teeth, wondering what had attracted Liam.

I wasn't ugly. I wasn't beautiful either. I was just—me. Dark hair, blue eyes, nothing special. I was taller than Beth, but below average in height. I leaned toward the healthier side of curvy rather than skinny. I had a scar above my right eyebrow from falling and hitting my head when I was a child. My ears were lopsided, so I usually wore my hair down, although Beth laughed when I told her that and said the only one who ever noticed was me. She was probably right, but still, I did it.

I padded into my bedroom, noting it was still early. The kids wouldn't be up for another hour or so, and Liam wasn't arriving until nine.

Liam.

Despite the teasing with Beth about a single brother for me, he was unexpected. Larger-than-life. The moment I'd opened the

41

door and our eyes met, something had shifted in my world. When his hand touched mine, I felt grounded—steady. Safe. His sheer size was enough to boggle my mind. He towered over me, filled the doorway, and crowded me as he went past. Yet, somehow, I wanted closer. He told me that his size often frightened people, but I hadn't been scared at all. In fact, if anyone took the time to look closer, to look into his eyes, they would know they had nothing to fear. His gaze was warm and gentle. His voice low and kind. And when he looked at me? I felt a tingle simply recalling the flare of desire I had felt and the way his expression returned it.

He was amazing with the kids. Lucy adored him as much as she adored Ronan. Maybe more, as if sensing a different sort of relationship with him. It was astonishing how much she resembled him with her coloring. The dark hair and hazel eyes matched his. I had always thought she looked like me with her facial features. I had searched more than once, seeing only echoes of Alan in her. The turn of her mouth when displeased, the small ears that hugged her head and were perfectly symmetrical. But he had sandy-colored hair and hazel eyes—although his had been flat, not vibrant like Lucy's. He was tall and slim. She had none of those similarities, and thank God, none of his exacting, critical personality. She was my little sunshine, loved everyone, and woke with a smile every day. She was the thing that had kept me going since Alan walked away. She gave me the strength to push forward.

Everything about Liam was the direct opposite of Alan. He exuded warmth and care. He was open with his feelings and expressed them easily. He made no secret of his feelings toward me.

Last night, after pizza, the kids crashed early after their full day. Liam and Ronan had left with promises of returning in the morning not long after the kids fell asleep. We said our goodbyes in separate rooms for privacy. Liam had pulled me into his arms.

"Go to bed and get some rest," he murmured. "Don't be sitting up all night talking to Beth about how amazing I am," he teased.

I slapped his chest. "I was going to tell her you were bossy. High-handed."

He chuckled. "When it comes to you, I am." He pressed a kiss to my mouth that was far too short for my liking. I tried to lengthen it, but he shook his head. "None of that, Sweet Pea, or I won't be leaving."

"Sweet Pea?"

He smiled and tucked a lock of hair behind my ear. "You smell like a garden of flowers. There's one note stronger than the others. It reminds me of one of my favorite flowers."

"Sweet peas?" I guessed.

He nodded. "You got it. And it suits you."

"I don't think I've ever had a nickname before."

He kissed me again, this time a little longer and a little harder. "You'll find lots of firsts with me. I promise you that."

Then he left, and, surprisingly, Beth and I did go to bed. We were both exhausted.

I shook my head to clear my musings and dressed with care. Meeting his family today, even as Beth's friend, was nerve-racking. I picked a pretty sundress I got on sale last year, sliding it over my head. It was summery and light, scattered with flowers on a soft blue background, and I rarely had an opportunity to wear it. I added a short-sleeved sweater in case I got chilly and headed to the kitchen to get coffee. I was going to need it today.

Liam arrived before Ronan, bringing with him his smile and calmness. He poured himself a cup of coffee, bounced Lucy on his knee, and listened to Evan talk about an idea he had for a Lego building.

"I think my mom was going to pull out all the kits she had of ours. Maybe we can build something while we're there," he told Evan, who grinned widely.

"Awesome." He stood and headed to his room to get ready.

Beth stood, looking pretty in a soft green dress. Her hair was a mass of corkscrew curls around her face, and she smiled, although I knew she was nervous. She held out her hand to Lucy.

"Come on, Lucy-loo. I'll help you get dressed."

"I want to wear my pink dress."

Beth met my gaze with a wink. "Which one?"

"With the flowers."

"Okay. One pink dress with the flowers, as soon as you brush your teeth."

Lucy looked up at Liam. "You stay, right?"

He nodded. "I'll be right here."

She slid from his lap and took Beth's hand. "Otay!"

"You want me to find her swimsuit?" Beth asked.

"I packed it and Evan's in a bag."

"You girls should bring yours too. The pool is great at the Hub. Warm."

"Maybe next time," Beth murmured. "We'll watch the kids today."

She left, and Liam shifted closer, closing his hand over mine on the table. "Hey."

I smiled at him. "Hi."

He leaned in, brushing his mouth over my lips. "Hi." He ran his nose over mine affectionately. "There's no need to be nervous. My family is great."

"I know. It's a big deal for Beth today. I want it to go well for her. She adores Ronan, so she wants to make a good impression. Me too, I guess, so they think we're okay."

"Hey." He slid his hand under my chin, making me look at him. "You're *more* than okay. You're perfect. They're going to love you, and Lucy, too."

My nerves got the better of me. "It's not as important, though, but I don't want to embarrass you or Beth."

He stood, frowning, and tugged my hand, leading me to my bedroom. He shut the door behind us and turned to look at me.

"Today is just as important for me." He drew in a deep breath. "I know you're going as Beth's friend, Paige, but you're also going as my date. I'm introducing you and Lucy to my family as mine. Both of you."

I felt my eyes widen. "Wh-what?"

He stepped closer, wrapping his arms around me. "Unless you tell me no, as of today, my family will know you're part of my life."

"But it's so..."

"Fast?" He finished. "Yes. Right? Yes." He looked down, brushing his fingers over my cheek. "Don't you feel how right it is, Sweet Pea?"

"What if you change your mind?"

He laughed, bending down and pressing a kiss to my mouth. "Not happening. When I make up my mind, I'm all in. And I am all in about you, baby. You and my little munchkin."

"Oh," I breathed out, unsure how to react. I wanted to throw my arms around his neck and kiss him until we were both breathless. To tell him I felt the exact same way. But I knew I had to remain calm.

"We'll take this as slow as you need. I know we have a lot to talk about, to learn about each other, but none of it is going to change what I'm feeling. How I know that we'll grow."

"I snore," I burst out.

He chuckled, ghosting his lips over my head. "So do I."

"I hog the covers."

"I'll keep you so warm, you won't need any."

"I babble when I get nervous."

He nibbled on my ear. "Like now?"

I swallowed. "I want this, Liam. I want you. I'm just—"

He cut me off with his mouth. His kiss was hard, sweet, and all too brief.

"Just nothing. We'll figure it out."

"Momma!" Little fists banged on the door. "Look at my dress!"

Liam chuckled, lifting my chin and meeting my eyes. "Mine?" he whispered.

My anxiety eased from my body, leaving me relaxed. "Yes."

His grin was wide, and his eyes danced with happiness. "Then let's go meet my family."

Liam's family was warm and welcoming. Not a single person blinked as he introduced me as "*his* Paige." They all opened their arms to Lucy, who charmed them with her smile, sweet voice, and affectionate nature. His father, Aiden, hugged me so hard and lifted me right off my feet, exclaiming his sons had excellent taste in their partners.

It was obvious they were all close. Paul and Jeremy introduced me to their girlfriends, Kim and Diane. They were friendly and approachable, smiling at my wonder.

"We're pretty new too," Kim whispered. "It's still overwhelming!"

Diane made me laugh. "But what a family. The DNA." She waved her hand in front of her face. "Am I right?"

I had to agree.

Still, my head spun from it all.

The food, the people, the laughter. The love.

My God, the *love*.

It was all around us. In conversations, laced into the teasing, loud in its joy at the huge gathering, which I was shocked to discover wasn't the entire family.

I could only imagine.

The men were handsome, kind, and loving. The lovely women fussed over their grown children and paid special attention to Evan and Lucy, showering them with attention and praise. More than once, I had to blink away the veil of moisture that gathered in my eyes. I had never experienced anything like it. At one point, I slipped from the room, having to tamp down the wave of emotion as I watched Aiden and Cami sit with Lucy. She talked to them animatedly, one hand on Aiden's cheek as she made sure he was listening. And he was—pure rapture at whatever bit of news she was sharing written on his face. She'd never known family outside of Beth and Evan. She had never experienced anything like this before now. Neither had I.

Liam found me only a moment later, coming into the room and enfolding me in his embrace.

"Too much, Sweet Pea?"

"Too wonderful," I sniffled.

He cupped my face. "I don't know your past, Paige, but I can promise you a different future. One where you're surrounded by love like this."

I wrapped my hand around his wrist. "How can you be so certain?"

He shrugged. "I can't explain it, but it doesn't make it any less real or amazing."

I shut my eyes as he leaned his forehead to mine. "You take my breath away," I admitted.

"You do the same to me."

He held me for a few moments, his warmth and strength calming me.

"You ready to go back out there? I promised Lucy she could help me plant a few things, and I want to show you the compound. And have you see my house."

"Yes."

I wandered through Liam's house, smiling. It was so...*Liam*. Lots of windows, a large patio with big chairs to sit on. Inside, the windows flooded the house with light and warmth. Open concept, it was simply furnished with large, masculine furniture. The kitchen was modern, with clean lines and stone work surfaces. He told me he liked to cook, and I could see him in here, chopping and stirring as he created a meal. The two extra bedrooms were a good size. He obviously used one as an office, and the other was empty aside from a double bed that faced the window with the lovely view of the trees. His bedroom was slate blue and white, the two colors playing off each other, creating a bright space. His bathroom held a separate shower and the largest freestanding soaker tub I had ever seen. The window was set higher and had some sort of tint so you couldn't see in, but your view out was unobstructed and it overlooked the water. I could only imagine how relaxing it was to sit and look out on that vista.

He came in behind me, encircling my waist and pulling me back against him. "You like?"

"Hmm. Much. Our tub is pretty small, and I rarely get the chance to use it."

"You can come use this one. I'll join you. Wash your back and stuff."

"Stuff?" I teased.

"Oh, baby. Lots and lots of *stuff*," he promised, nipping my neck.

My laughter turned into a low whimper as he moved his mouth up my skin to my ear, nuzzling at it.

"Where is Lucy?"

"Digging in my garden. She instructed me to go 'get Momma' so you could see her handiwork."

"You shouldn't let her order you around."

He laughed and kissed my neck, then spun me in his arms. "I am happy to take orders from the munchkin or her momma."

I lifted one eyebrow in challenge. "Oh yeah? Then kiss——"

His mouth was on mine before I could finish.

I liked this order-issuing thing.

Liam carried Lucy into the house and watched as I tugged off her shoes, wiped her face and hand with a damp cloth, and tucked her in.

"You don't want to put her nightgown on?" he asked.

I shook my head. "She needs a bath. She can have one in the morning, and I'll make her bed up fresh. She's got a layer of dirt everywhere."

"She did enjoy gardening."

I glanced over my shoulder with a grin. "Is that what you'd call it? I'd say more digging as deep for worms as she could."

He laughed. "She did like the way they wiggled."

I straightened and kissed her forehead. "Sleep well, my baby." I brushed my hand over her curls then headed to Liam.

"She had such a good day."

He pulled me close. "What about her momma? She have a good day too?"

"Yes."

"Good."

He followed me to the living room, and we sat close together on the sofa.

"My family liked you. Very much. And they adored Lucy."

"They were pretty amazing," I replied. "Are they always that open?"

"Open?" he repeated.

"Well, you bring a stranger and her daughter they've never heard about to brunch, announce we're together, and none of them batted an eye. Or is that something you do a lot?" I asked, partially teasing, partially serious.

He shook his head and turned to face me fully. He slid his hands along my leg, gripping my knees lightly, his thumbs stroking over the skin.

"First off, no, I have never taken anyone home. Not since university. Second, they have heard about you. From Ronan. From me. I'm close to my parents and immediate family. I've talked about you and Lucy this past while, not hiding anything. You'll figure out pretty fast, I'm an open book. When I feel something, I show it. If I'm upset, I'll tell you why. If I'm happy, I'll share the cause." His hands tightened on my skin. "If I care, I will tell you."

"Were you always so, ah, expressive?"

He shook his head. "No, I was pretty uptight when I was younger. I held myself back a lot. There was a girl I liked in university. We met first year, and I was interested in her. But I was Mr. Cool and played the field. But there was something there, and finally, I got my head out of my ass and asked her out. We were great together, and I began to care about her. Really care. But I was young and stupid, and I didn't tell her."

"What happened?"

"She went home for winter break." He paused, swallowing. "She died in a skiing accident."

"Oh, Liam," I whispered.

"She knew I liked her, but not how much. She went home to Alberta, and I never saw her again. I was gonna tell her when she got back. I even bought her a special present. I always regretted not saying the words. Not telling her *how* important she was to me. She died not knowing how much I cared."

For a moment, he was silent, then he cleared his throat. "I swore I would never let that happen again. From then on, I became really open. I hugged my friends. Told my family I loved them. Started to talk about things." He met my eyes. "I decided if I ever loved someone, I would let them know. Say the words. Prove it with actions. Make them certain they were important."

He slid his hands up, covering mine on my lap. "You are important, Paige. I know it sounds crazy and it's only been a short time, but I'm crazy about you. And Lucy. I don't want to scare you, but I meant what I said earlier. I'm all in, Sweet Pea. Completely and totally all in."

Then his mouth was on mine.

He kissed the way he did everything. With passion and feeling. He cupped my face, his callused fingers gentle on my skin as he showed me how he was feeling. I wrapped my arms around his neck, pulling myself closer. With a low groan, he tugged me on his lap, the kiss becoming harder. Deeper. More consuming. I had never felt like this about a man. Never wanted someone as much as I wanted him. I couldn't get close enough. I wanted to feel his skin on mine, taste him all over.

"Stay," I pleaded against his lips.

He didn't respond, but stood, taking me with him. He carried me to my bedroom, shutting the door behind him. He set me on my feet, looking down at me, his breathing harsh, his eyes dark with desire. "Do you need to check on Lucy or do anything else?"

"I-I should peek in on her."

"Do it now, because once I start with you, I'm not going to be able to stop."

He opened the door, and I sidled past him, feeling the strength in his body. The thickness of him that proved how much he wanted me.

I looked back at him. "You better be naked when I get back."

"You better brace yourself," he replied, lowering his hand to his zipper.

I hurried down the hall, checking on Lucy. I already knew she was fine. Once she was out, she rarely ever woke up, and she slept soundly. I peeked in on Evan. He was asleep, one arm flung out. His headphones were on, so I knew he was good for the night as well.

Then I stopped in the bathroom and gave myself a few moments to calm down and get ready.

I pulled off my clothes, splashed some water on my overheated skin, and tugged on my robe, wishing it were a pretty, sexy silk one instead of a well-worn, no-longer-fuzzy-in-patches one.

Then I decided it probably didn't matter. I had a feeling once I went back into my bedroom, it would disappear pretty fast.

I took a deep breath and headed down the hall to where Liam was waiting.

CHAPTER SIX

LIAM

She was beautiful and nervous as she stepped into the room, shutting the door quietly behind her. Her hair gleamed under the lights, the glints of red shimmering in the dark tresses. Her eyes were wide with worry and desire, and her fingers clenched and unclenched on the belt of her worn robe.

She needed a new one. New furniture. A more comfortable bed. I was barely going to fit on this double, but for now, I would make it work. I didn't care how sore my back and legs would be tomorrow. I wanted her too much to care. And soon, I would make sure she had everything she needed to be comfortable, too.

I stood, wearing only my black boxers. My desire was evident, the bulge thick and aching, tenting the front. Her eyes widened farther as I approached, offering her my hand. She came to me willingly and sighed as I settled my mouth on hers. I loved the little sound of contentment she made every time our lips touched. I stepped back, taking her with me until my legs hit the mattress. Breaking our kiss, I sat down, looking up at her as I slid my hands to the knot at her waist.

"Can I?" I asked.

Her breathing stuttered.

"Talk to me."

"I'm-I'm not perfect, Liam. I have stretch marks from Lucy. I'm not—"

I cut her off. "You're beautiful."

I untied the knot and reached up, pushing the robe off her shoulders. It fell to the floor with a low thump, and I caught my breath. Her skin was creamy and smooth. Her breasts full with deep rosy-colored nipples that begged for my mouth. She was curvy with a sweet indentation at her waist that flared to full hips. Her legs were slender, and I wanted them wrapped around me.

Now.

I kissed her stomach, ghosting my lips over the tiny silvery lines that feathered along her hips. I slid my hands around her, spreading them wide on her back as I used my mouth to relay how lovely she was to me. I whispered words of adoration to her skin, following a path to her heavy breasts, taking a nipple into my mouth and sucking. Her head fell back as I paid equal attention to the other side, then ran my mouth down, going lower, burying my face and nuzzling into the heat between her legs. She whimpered as I worshiped her with my mouth for the next moments, then pulled her down on top of me on the mattress. Our mouths met as our hands explored each other, discovering and learning. She was ticklish under her ribs. She loved having her nipples sucked and nibbled. She shuddered as my fingers explored her cleft, running along the slit to her ass and back. I groaned at the scrape of her teeth on my neck, the feel of her hand stroking me. She pulled off my boxers, and my cock sprang free, hot, heavy, and already leaking for her.

"I want to taste you," she murmured.

I rolled her over. "Next time. The second your mouth is on me, I'll come. I want to be inside you the first time."

"I'm on the pill."

"I have condoms."

"No," she whispered. "Just you."

I settled between her legs, gliding my cock along her entrance. She was hot, wet, and ready. I was aching with want. Needing to be inside her. She reached down, guiding my head to her entrance.

"Please."

I snapped my hips, burying myself inside her. Her eyes went wide and her back arched. She made a low, sexy noise in the back of her throat. I held myself still, the urge to thrust and claim overpowering. But I wanted this to be good for her. I wanted her writhing in pleasure under me. Screaming my name. Quietly, since we didn't want visitors.

I waited until I felt her muscles relax and her hips move restlessly, and I began to pump inside her. Slowly at first, then as she wrapped her legs around me harder and her *pleases* began, I went faster. I gripped the edge of the mattress for purchase. Her nails sank into my shoulders. I felt the material under my fingers give way as I took her. The bed shifted, the frame creaking. I kissed her as my body began to shake, the sweat gathering between my shoulder blades and my forehead getting damp. Our skin slid together, the friction hot and delicious as our bodies moved as if we'd done this a thousand times. She fit me perfectly. She was perfect.

She stiffened, her muscles gripping my cock, squeezing it hard, and she met my eyes, the ecstasy evident as she shook beneath me. I covered her cries with my mouth, groaning into her as I found my release. We moved in the aftershocks, now slower, our bodies not wanting to let go of the moment, the pleasure, or the intimate embrace.

Until, finally, we were both spent.

I kissed her one last time and rolled off her, lying on my side, and pulling her into my arms.

She nestled against me, her breathing ragged, her skin cooling rapidly after our exertions. I felt around for the blanket I had seen earlier and pulled it over her, holding her close.

There was so much I wanted to say to her. So many words to share and plans to make. But after only a few moments, I heard the snores she warned me about. Little, breathy snorts of air that made me smile.

I pressed a kiss to her head and tucked her closer. We'd talk later. Right now, she was exactly where she should be. Safe and resting in my arms.

I planned on that being where she stayed the rest of her life.

Monday was a great day. Waking up with Paige beside me in the early hours of the morning was the perfect way to start it off. I opened my eyes, meeting the soft blue of her gaze, and for a moment, neither of us spoke. I cupped her cheek, and she covered my hand with hers, holding it close to her skin. I leaned in and kissed her gently.

"Last night was incredible," I whispered.

"Three a.m. was pretty spectacular too," she replied with a little grin.

I glanced at the clock and pulled her closer. "Five a.m. is gonna be even better," I assured her.

She giggled, sliding her hand up to cradle my head.

Five a.m. turned out to be my favorite.

A short while later, she walked me to the door, neither of us speaking until we got outside.

"I'll see you tonight," I said, tucking a strand of hair behind her ear.

She slipped her hands into the pockets of her robe. "Okay."

"Be ready for seven?"

She nodded, and I pulled her into my arms, kissing her goodbye. I held her close, hating to leave her but knowing I had to. "This is just the start, Sweet Pea."

Her arms tightened, and I pressed a kiss to her head. I headed to the truck, passing Ronan and Beth. I high-fived my brother and got into the truck, laughing. I was certain we were both wearing the same ridiculously happy expressions. The Callaghan brothers were both having a great Monday.

All day, Paige was on my mind. Everything seemed to remind me of her. The coffee I sipped wasn't as good as the cup she made me. She got the cream just right. I watched a mother tugging impatiently on the arm of her child as they walked, and I thought about the patience I saw Paige show Lucy, and I marveled at how she did it on her own. I saw a couple walking hand in hand, and I hoped that would be Paige and me soon. Together, out for a walk, wanting that connection of our hands pressing together.

I sent her a text midmorning, letting her know I was thinking of her and looking forward to our date. Not long after, I stopped by my favorite nursery to place an order for a job. As I walked through with Michelle, choosing plants and bushes, the scent of sweet peas hit me and I grinned at the huge wall of them climbing up the fence, the varied, pretty colors a muted canvas of petals.

An idea hit me. "You do flower arrangements as well, right?" I asked Michelle.

"Yes. You need one?"

"Yeah, I do."

"Do you want to take it or delivery?"

I recalled my mom getting flowers from my dad. He often brought them home, but he had them delivered at times as well. My mom always loved that because it was so unexpected. "A surprise to brighten her day," my dad always said. I had a feeling Paige never got surprises like that. She would love it.

"Delivered. Can you do it today?"

"For you? Of course."

"Can you add some sweet peas into the mix? I want lots of fragrance. Roses, fuchsia, maybe some lilacs?"

"Any lilies?"

"Yes. Make it spectacular."

"And fragrant. Gotcha. Must be a special lady."

I grinned. "Very."

Around five, I was heading toward the office to make a few calls and change for tonight when my phone buzzed. I read Paige's message, frowning at her words of having to cancel tonight. Then Ronan called, his voice thick with anger.

"Can you come to the house?"

I knew he meant Paige's place. "What's wrong?"

"Evan got pushed around this afternoon. Some bullies at school."

"Fuck," I swore, immediately turning the truck around to head that way. "Does he need to go to the hospital?"

"No, but he needs us."

"I'm on my way. I'm about thirty minutes with traffic."

"I hate to ask, but—"

I cut him off. "Paige already canceled. I'll bring dinner. We'll help Evan tonight."

"Thanks, Liam. I owe you."

"Nope," I replied. "This is family."

We both spoke at the same time. "It's what we do."

Our father and uncles had drummed that motto into our heads all our lives. Family came first. Always.

I hung up, shaking my head. Evan was a good kid, and he didn't deserve to be picked on. Paige loved him like a brother of her own. She would be upset. Beth would be beside herself with worry.

I gunned the engine, changing lanes.

Not the evening I had planned.

I arrived, stepping from the truck and approaching Evan and Ronan, who were sitting on the steps. Evan's face was a mess, but he was being brave. I had him tell me what happened, and as he explained, I felt the anger build at these faceless little shits who picked on a kid less fortunate than themselves. My father had always told us, especially given our size, it was our job to watch out for those who couldn't defend themselves.

"You protect, never hurt," he said over and again. "You help people. You never tear them down."

I sat next to Evan and Ronan as he described what occurred. The way the boys surrounded him and why. All because he told the truth about meeting our family. They called him a liar and pushed him around, kicking his crutches out so he fell.

I met Ronan's eyes over his head. My brother wasn't going to let this rest. "Beth is going to talk to the principal," he said. "Again."

I nodded in understanding. It wouldn't help if she'd already tried. I clapped Evan on the shoulder. "I brought Chinese for dinner. Ronan said it was your favorite. I got you extra spring rolls."

A real smile broke out on his face. "Awesome."

"You go inside and wash up. We'll be right there."

He got up and went inside, his limp more pronounced than ever. No doubt, he was aching head to toe from his fall earlier. I headed to the truck, getting the bags of food.

"I'm going to contact the teacher that Evan likes. The one who was having the discussion about BAM today," Ronan said.

"What do you have in mind?"

"I think one of our company community visits is in order."

"The power of BAM, you mean?"

He nodded.

"I'll call Bentley and rally the troops. You know he'll support this one hundred and ten percent."

Ronan nodded, looking grim. "That's what I'm counting on."

Paige looked surprised to see me, but she accepted my kiss, her hug tight as I pulled her close. I dropped a kiss on her head. "It's okay, Sweet Pea. We're here. We're going to figure this out."

"I'm glad you're here," she admitted. "But I'm not sure what you can do except talk to Evan."

I slipped my fingers under her chin and smiled. "Trust me on this. There is a lot we can do."

She looked confused, but she went along with it. "Okay."

I dropped another kiss to her mouth. "Good."

"My flowers," she whispered. "They are so beautiful, Liam. I've never gotten flowers before."

"Ever?"

"Not once," she confirmed. "I was sure they were for Beth or the wrong address," she admitted. "Until this happened, I couldn't stop smiling."

"I always want you smiling."

She hugged me again, her arms tight around my waist. I wrapped her close, letting her know I was there and she wasn't alone in this or anything else.

"I'm here," I said quietly. "Not going anywhere."

Her sigh was shaky and low. "Good."

We made Evan smile during dinner. The spring rolls helped. Lucy was attentive, sitting between Evan and me, fussing over his "boo-boos," which she thought he got after his crutch slipped. She helped him with extra plum sauce and made sure he had lots of crunchy noodles on his chow mein, which meant a pile over his entire plate. He ate it all, not once impatient with her. After dinner, the girls went for a walk to get ice cream, while Ronan and I talked more with Evan.

"You going to school tomorrow, bud?" Ronan asked.

Evan shifted in his seat. "Yeah. I can't let them win, right?"

Ronan nodded. "Right. Just be careful. I have an idea that might help, but I need a couple days to pull it together, okay?"

"Okay." Evan paused. "Does this have something to do with asking for Mr. Humphries's email?"

"Yeah."

"Okay, Ronan. I trust you." He looked at me. "You too, Liam."

I pulled him in for a fast hug. "Good man."

We ate ice cream after the girls got home. I sat on the steps while Paige put Lucy to bed, and Ronan and Beth stayed with Evan. Paige came outside, sitting beside me. I slipped an arm around her shoulder and pulled her close.

"Lucy settle okay?"

"Once she was sure her unicorn was tucked in too, yes." She chuckled. "That thing you won her is as big as she is."

"Bigger," I agreed.

"Sorry about our date."

"Nothing to be sorry for. Ronan says he's coming over tomorrow. We can go out then."

"Oh, ah—"

I cut off her objections. "They'll look after Lucy, and it gives them some alone time. I want to take you out."

"All right."

I pressed a kiss to her head. "So enthusiastic."

She laughed and snuggled closer. "I just feel guilty."

"Doing something for yourself, you mean?"

"Yes."

"I told you, your life is changing, Paige. What happened before is the past."

"Sometimes that lingers," she whispered.

"Your ex," I said.

I felt her nod against my chest. I waited, but she didn't say anything.

"You don't have any family?" I asked.

"No. My parents split when I was little. My mom died when I started university. It was just her and me. I never saw my father aside from a few pictures. He was older than my mother. He passed a few years before she did."

"Was she ill?"

"Yes." She swallowed. "We weren't, ah, close. I think she always blamed me for my father leaving us. I mean, she was nice and treated me okay, but there wasn't any affection, and she encouraged me to leave as early as possible. She always treated me like a friend or a little sister, not a mom. I learned how to do things on my own pretty fast."

"Sounds lonely."

"It was. I always swore my kids would know how much they were loved."

"Lucy knows."

"I hope so."

"Hey." I waited until she met my eyes. "You are an amazing mother. In fact, you're the whole package, Paige. Loving, caring, beautiful, sexy—" I stopped at the subtle shake of her head.

"You brush off my compliments all the time." I narrowed my eyes. "Between your mother and your ex, you have no idea how special you are, do you?"

She played with the hem of the sweater she was wearing. "I-I don't know how to answer that." She swallowed. "Alan was very critical. I mean, when we dated, he seemed uptight at times, but once we were married, he became controlling and, ah, very vocal about my shortcomings."

"Your shortcomings?" I repeated. I didn't really want to have this conversation here, sitting outside, but since it had come up, I decided we needed to address it.

"I was too slow, I didn't keep the house tidy enough, my clothes didn't fit me the way they should since I was, ah, fat. Nothing ever pleased him. He constantly compared me to his friends' and coworkers' wives. They were prettier, sexier. Thinner." She snorted. "Taller too, not that I could do much about that."

"Yet you stayed with him."

"I didn't have anywhere else to go. He had taken over my life without me even realizing it."

"Lucy?" I asked.

"All his friends' wives were getting pregnant. He always wanted to keep up the appearance of a perfect, happy couple." She sighed. "It was like a competition. Someone got a new car, he had to have one. They got the latest cell, he bought a better one. They remodeled their bathroom with a soaker tub, he got a hot tub. Always more. It was never enough." She shook her head. "Nothing, especially me, was ever enough." She rested her chin on her hand and canted her head toward me. "He wanted a baby too. I thought maybe if we had kids, he'd relax. Be happy. Be a family."

"Didn't work, did it?"

"No. I had a hard pregnancy. I was sick all the time, and he complained. He never came to a doctor's appointment with me. He told me I was making it up—faking being sick to get out of cleaning the house or cooking or going to one of his stupid work events." She shared a small smile. "I have to admit, I didn't miss those boring things."

"What happened?" I asked.

"When the ultrasound showed Lucy's arm not growing properly, he freaked. Blamed me. Said he wasn't going to have a baby that wasn't perfect in his life. He ranted and raved. Threw things. Stormed out." She shifted, wrapping her arms around her knees and drawing in on herself.

"The next day, he came home and told me to get an abortion. I was shocked at his callousness and pointed out it was far too late for that, and even if it weren't, I wasn't harming my child. He said we'd have to put it up for adoption, then, and tell people it had died. *It.* He kept referring to my baby as an it. My beautiful little girl as an it—as if she were nothing. All because of a missing limb."

I had to keep my hands tight to my sides. I wanted to punch something to release the anger I was feeling. What a bastard.

"I told him to go fuck himself. He walked out. The next time we saw each other was across the table with our lawyers. I accepted his settlement, he signed away his rights, and I never looked back. I found a job, had Lucy, and eventually, met Beth. We became each other's family."

I knew there was more to her story than she was saying. More details, more fears, and more trauma. But I also knew she was getting near the end of her rope. Her voice had become thicker, and she curled in on herself, as if warding off the emotion.

I had to touch her. To hold her close and break the chains of her past. Turning, I scooped her up, settling her on my lap.

"Your ex was an asshole. A complete and total bastard. He didn't deserve you or Lucy. And he was wrong on so many levels, Sweet Pea."

She looked up at me, furrowing her brow.

"He was no better than the kids who bullied Evan. You were vulnerable, and instead of helping, he kicked you when you were down. All the words he said to you? All the nasty names and the neglect? That's on him. Not you. Something I've found is that bullies hate themselves and take it out on people around them. He picked on you because you were everything he was not."

I held her closer. "You are beautiful, Paige. You're warm, kind, an awesome mother, an incredible human being."

She opened her mouth then closed it.

"And you're sexy. So sexy, it boggles my mind. Your eyes are like the sky on a lazy summer's day, the blue soft and warm. I love everything about you. How thick your hair is and how it feels between my fingers. Your skin is like silk, and I love to touch it. I love how you smile. It lights up my chest. Your curves drive me wild. And I love the fact that you're shorter. You're easier to pick up and carry around."

That earned me a little giggle, the corner of her mouth quirking in amusement.

"I can't erase what he said, but I can tell you this. It was all bull-shit. To make himself feel better, he had to make you feel bad. And his behavior over Lucy? I would like to find him and beat him senseless." I paused. "But in the end, I won, because I got you and her." I ran a finger down her cheek. "I plan to never let you go."

"Liam," she whispered.

"How I feel won't change. How I treat you won't change. I'm not him." I sucked in a deep breath. "I know it's scary for you, Paige, but I'm going to lay it on the line. I love you. It's as simple and complex as that. I don't care if it's been a week, a month, or a year. I love you. You and Lucy are going to be my world. Some-how, I'm going to prove that to you."

For a moment, there was silence. She blinked.

"You don't have to say it back. I'll wait for you. Anything you need is yours. All you have to do is ask."

"Anything?" she asked, her voice shaking.

"Anything."

"Hold me," she pleaded.

I wrapped her closer, and she flung her arms around my neck. I breathed in her flowery scent, drawing it deep into my lungs.

There was so much I didn't say. So much I didn't tell her. That I planned to marry her. Make Lucy mine. Keep them both safe and happy always. I wanted to tell her she would never worry about money, love, or anything again. She would have it all as long as she was mine.

Instead, I let my embrace soothe her. I had a feeling she'd been needing this for a long time.

She pressed her lips to my ear, her wet cheek warm against my skin. "I love you too, Liam Callaghan. So very much."

My eyes filled with tears, and I pulled her closer.

That was what I needed.

CHAPTER SEVEN
LIAM

Paige cried herself out in my arms, her sobs muffled in my chest as I held her tight. I didn't try to hush her. I didn't croon and tell her everything was okay. She needed to let it out, and as much as it hurt me to hear her sobs, I needed to let her. When the last of the painful sounds faded away and she drooped in my embrace, I brushed the hair away from her damp skin and peered down at her.

"Hey."

"I'm—"

"Don't say you're sorry. You never have to be sorry about showing your emotions with me. I'm here for you."

"You really are," she murmured in wonder.

I stood, taking her with me.

"What are you doing?"

"We're going to bed. You need to sleep, and I need to keep holding you for a while."

"I'm too heavy—"

Again, I cut her off.

"No," I stated firmly. "You aren't."

Ronan and Beth were sitting on the sofa, talking as we went in. Beth looked startled and began to stand, but I shook my head and kept walking. I knew Paige wouldn't want Beth to see her so upset. I carried Paige to the bathroom and set her on her feet.

"I'll be waiting."

In her room, I pulled back the blankets and sat on the bed, wondering how to convince her to let me buy her a bigger, more comfortable one. I heard Ronan and Beth head downstairs, no doubt to give us some privacy, and a few moments later, Paige came into her room, looking tired and worn out, already wearing a long nightshirt, the material thin. I held out my hand, and she let me tug her close. "Eeyore?" I asked with a grin, tracing over the faded image.

"From Evan a few years ago. Beth took him shopping at Christmas. He picked it. He says I look like this in the mornings before coffee."

I chuckled. "Brothers—even added ones. Always the same."

I patted the mattress, and she sat against the headboard, looking at me nervously. I sat across from her, our knees pressed together.

"Do you trust me, Paige?"

"Yes."

"Have I ever been anything but truthful with you?"

"No. You're a very honest person."

"I want to do a little word readjustment."

"Word readjustment?"

"Yes." I tapped her forehead. "I want to get rid of some of the words you have up here." At her frown, I added, "Just a few."

"Okay?" she said, making it sound more like a question.

"Your ex—he called you heavy?"

She swallowed. "Yes."

"I call you curvy. Perfect." I paused. "Far better words. And the truth. See? Like that. Hit me with another word he liked to use."

"Plain."

"Beautiful." Emphasizing my reply, I lifted her hand and kissed her knuckles.

"Slow and lazy."

"Methodical," I corrected, pressing her hand to my cheek.

"Stupid and boring."

"Intelligent and cautious," I insisted, placing a kiss to her palm.

"Gullible."

"Kindhearted."

"Weak."

"Strong. Holy shit, baby, so strong," I replied steadfastly.

She dragged in a long breath. "Frigid and unresponsive."

I shook my head furiously. "*Passionate and sexy*. You walk in the room, I get a boner. Thinking about us together, I get a hard-on in the truck. I swear to God, he's trying to take the wheel. It's quite embarrassing."

Her lips twitched, and I knew she was starting to relax.

"Your ex probably had a dick the size of my thumb," I added. "And no idea how to use it."

Her eyes widened, and I saw the flare of amusement in them. I also saw how tired she looked, and I knew I had made my point. But she spoke again.

"Placid," she said.

"Wrong again. Sweet." I held up my finger. "Also, a lake in New York. Nice place, I hear. As well as a famous opera singer." I pursed my lips. "Or maybe that was Plácido. I always get them confused."

She bit back her smile. "Wan."

I didn't even bother to correct that one. "Ah, the beloved ruler of coffee. Wan Valdez. A favorite of mine."

That did it. She let out a little giggle, the sound making me grin.

"Does this mean we're done?" she asked.

I met her eyes. "For now. As long as you believe me. He was a walking pack of lies and hate. I want to take every nasty word he said and replace it with a positive one until they're all gone. I've got all night." I crossed my legs. "Rest of my life, too."

"You've made your point. I do believe you."

"Then stop letting that voice—his voice—influence you. You are amazing, Paige. If you were any of those things he accused you of being, you would have crumbled. You didn't. You pushed forward, and you have a wonderful little girl as awesome as you are. Good friends. Someone who is crazy about you and sees everything good and right in you. So does Beth. Ronan. My entire family. Pretty sure that outranks the asshole who walked away from you."

Her eyes were round. "It does."

"Let it go. Let everything he said go. Listen to *me*. Listen to my voice. Don't disregard my compliments when they're heartfelt and real. I think you're so close to perfect, it's scary."

A smile played on her lips, the heaviness of the past while starting to lift. It had with every response I had made to her whispered confessions. It was as if I were wiping them away one by one. "Close to?" she teased.

"Well, aside from the snoring and the babbling when nervous."

That earned me another smile as she recalled her words from the other day.

"A dick the size of your thumb?" She chuckled as I held it up, and she shook her head. "That's being generous."

It was my turn to laugh.

"And your cock trying to grab the wheel, Liam? You need to write a country song about that one."

"A number one hit, I bet."

She grinned. It was real, warm, and perfectly Paige. I leaned forward and kissed her. "My voice. Listen to my words. Not his."

"I'll try."

"I'll be around to remind you."

She cupped my cheek. "I like those words."

"Oh yeah?" I pulled her onto my lap. "Here are some more. I love you."

She cuddled close. "Those are the best." She looked up, her eyes no longer worried but peaceful.

"I love you, Liam."

She was right. They were the best.

PAIGE

I hung up from another work call and rolled my shoulders. I glanced at the clock and grimaced. It was barely noon, and I was exhausted. Yesterday's emotion with Evan then Liam had taken its toll, and although I had slept for over five hours, today, I felt drained.

Liam had left around five, and I had lain in bed, holding the pillow his head had rested on, and thought about his words. He was right—I had to stop hearing and feeling everything with the echo of Alan's nasty words, his anger. The boy I had fallen in love with wasn't the man who walked away from me. From Lucy. He was angry and twisted, a shadow of the person I'd thought he was.

He was my past.

Liam was my future.

A knock on the door roused me from my musings. Ronan was on the doorstep, his wide smile greeting me.

"Hi." I opened the door wider. "Beth isn't here."

He stepped in. "I know. I'm not here for her. I'm here for you."

"Sorry?"

"You need to call in sick for the rest of the afternoon. I have it on good authority that my brother is at his place in Port Albany working for the afternoon. I also know nothing would make him happier than a visit from you. A long, quiet evening with you. He brought Beth to me, so I'm bringing you to him."

"But Lucy—"

"All arranged. Beth isn't up to going out tonight with this Evan shit going on. We'll pick up Lucy and spend the evening. Liam will bring you home in the morning." He lifted his eyebrows, tapping his foot. "What are you waiting for?"

I threw my arms around his neck and hugged him. "Give me ten minutes."

"I went to the store and got you the things Beth said to pick up. Liam's favorite is pot roast, and Beth says yours is awesome."

My mind spun as I hurried away. "Okay," I called over my shoulder. They'd thought of everything.

Lucy would have a blast with Ronan, Beth, and Evan. I knew she'd be well cared for. And I got Liam. Alone.

My day just got brighter.

―――――――

Ronan was fairly quiet on the drive, although his phone was a constant barrage of noise. He got a lot of texts, which he ignored, and the calls were one-sided conversations thanks to the

Bluetooth he had in his ear. He was obviously planning something, and when he hung up from the last call, I glanced at him.

"Is all that about Evan?"

"Yeah."

I didn't ask any other questions. I knew he'd share when he was ready.

"How was Beth after I left this morning?" he asked.

"She was still upset, but calm. I haven't spoken to her to see how the meeting with the principal went."

He grunted. "About how she expected. No one is talking, and the other boys insist Evan fell on his own." He slammed his hand on the wheel. "I really hate bullies."

"I think he's been dealing with it for a while. Beth tries to get him to talk, but he never says anything. Some days, though..." I paused, and Ronan prompted me.

"Some days what?"

"Some days, he's quieter when he gets home. Goes right to his room. I think those are the days he's picked on more. I always try to cheer him up, get him to talk. He puts on a brave face, and I know he licks his wounds in private so Beth won't worry——"

"But she still does," he finished for me.

"Yes."

He glanced over at me as he slowed down at the gate to the houses. "She won't have to for much longer. He's not alone in this. I promise you." His gaze was intense and focused.

I smiled as I patted his arm. I knew he had something planned. "I'm glad she has you, Ronan. She and Evan."

He grunted. "I'm the lucky one."

He pulled into the driveway at Liam's. He grinned as he handed me the bag of groceries. "Tell Liam we're square now. See you in the morning." He winked and grinned, watching me walk to the door. Unsure what else to do, I knocked and waited. A case of nerves hit me. What if Liam wasn't happy to see me? Maybe he was too busy for an impromptu visit. I looked behind me where Ronan was waiting. Is that why he wasn't leaving?

I could hear Liam approaching the door, his voice carrying through the screen. "I heard your truck, little bro. Why are you knocking, and why aren't you—" He stopped in shock when he saw me, any doubt of his welcome evaporating when his smile broke out, wide and excited. He pushed open the door, reaching out and wrapping me in his arms. He lifted me right off my feet, the same way his dad had the other day.

"What a surprise!"

"A good one?" I asked breathlessly.

He set me down and cupped my face. "The best." He lowered his head, startling when Ronan honked the horn.

"We're even, bro!" Ronan shouted and began to back out of the driveway.

"You wish," Liam called back with a wide grin. He took the bag from my hand and peered inside. "You and dinner?"

I cleared my throat. "And the night too, if you want?"

He grabbed my hand, pulling me into the house. "If I want? Sweet Pea, you just made my entire week."

"You need to work," I gasped, trying to push him away. He had me crowded against the counter, his body pressing into mine.

He pushed closer, shaking his head. "What I need to do is kiss you again. Then take you to bed."

I pushed on his chest. "I didn't come here to interrupt your day. You have me for hours."

"Not enough time. I never get enough time with you."

I pointed to his office. "Work. Now. I'll make dinner and get it in the oven."

"I like you bossy."

I pointed to the hall. He pouted, which made me grin. "Now," I said firmly. "Or I'll call Ronan back and leave."

"You wouldn't." He narrowed his eyes.

I had to laugh. "No, I wouldn't, but please do your work or I'll feel guilty."

"Okay. But come find me as soon as you're done."

I headed to the kitchen and put the pot roast in the oven. It could cook slowly for the afternoon and leave me free to enjoy the found time and Liam. His kitchen was organized, and everything was easy to find. I wandered around his house, not surprised to find his bed neatly made and everything tidy. He was that sort of person. I stopped in his office door, studying him as he typed on the computer. He had a pencil shoved behind his ear and a drawing of something on his desk. His brow was furrowed as he glanced between the drawing and the screen. He noticed me in the doorway and reached out his hand.

I squealed a little when he pulled me into his lap, encircling me in one arm. He pressed a kiss to my neck.

"Something smells awesome."

"Pot roast."

That earned me a groan of approval. "I love pot roast."

"Ronan mentioned that." I looked at his drawing. "What are you doing?"

"This is a plan for a garden. I'm listing all the flowers and shrubs I need so I can price it out." He clicked another window that brought up a 3-D image of his drawing. "I drop the images in here." He tapped the paper drawing. "I use this when planting, but the customer gets to see my vision before I do all the work." He chuckled dryly. "Far easier to change in here than rip out plants and start again."

"Where is this?"

"A private home in Toronto. One of the old places that still has land. The woman inherited it from her grandparents, but they let it run wild and she isn't much of a gardener. I'm going to thin it out and add some easy to care for plants."

"Do you do a lot of private homes?"

"Yes. It's how I keep one set of crews employed. She wants a service package to maintain it. We do several properties that I've designed. We don't take on a client unless we've done the gardens or grounds. I keep it pretty exclusive." He chuckled. "There are a ton of companies that cut grass and weed gardens already. We make sure the gardens and landscaping we install look beautiful year after year."

"How many people do you employ?"

"About forty. I have a base in Toronto and one here. I do a lot of commercial work in both places, in between them as well. I have a manager in each location. I do all of the bids and design." He chuckled. "Only some install and no upkeep. That's what the young people are for. Perks of being an owner."

I looked around the room, spying some awards. "You're obviously talented."

"I love what I do. I'm lucky."

"Now who's brushing off compliments?" I teased.

He laughed, his arm tightening. "Touché, my girl. Touché."

He clicked save on his computer. "How about a walk on the beach? It's beautiful out, and I want to spend the rest of the afternoon with you."

"I'd love that."

He held out his hand. "Great."

CHAPTER EIGHT
PAIGE

I lifted my face to the sun, enjoying the breeze and the peace surrounding me. Liam's hand was wrapped securely around mine. The water lapped at my bare feet, the coolness feeling good between my toes. I glanced at Liam, my breath catching. He was dressed in jeans and a Henley, the material stretched tight over his chest. He'd rolled up his jeans, exposing his calves. He had surprisingly sexy legs. He wore sunglasses, which somehow highlighted the rugged features on his face. The wind lifted his hair, and he had a contented smile as we walked. Neither of us felt the need to fill the silence with conversation, and I was enjoying the tranquility. We reached an outcropping of rocks, the sand disappearing under the piles of boulders and jagged piles of stone.

"What's over there?" I pointed to a house on a low bluff that overlooked the water.

"Mr. Owens's place. Our property ends about three-quarters of the way across this stretch of rock. His begins. He's not exactly friendly."

"Oh?"

"He likes Ava, I think. He lets my mom visit on occasion. But he hates all the dads."

That surprised me. The BAM men were kind and helpful. "Why?"

"He was always standoffish. Intensely private. Once his wife died, he became more reclusive. Still, my family checked on him to make sure he was okay. Bentley made him an open offer if he ever wanted to sell his property. He even told him he could live there for as long as he wanted. He said no and got it into his head they were after the property and nothing else." Liam shook his head. "He chased my dad off once when he was taking him some meals my mom had made. He got out his shotgun and ordered him off."

"Oh my God!"

Liam shook his head. "It's old, has no bullets, and Mr. Owens could barely hold it. But since then, Ava is sort of the official go-between. He's not doing well, so she checks on him a lot. My dad arranged care for him that he thinks the hospital sends. If he knew it came from my family, he'd refuse, the stubborn old goat. At least that way, we know he has someone looking after him besides us."

"That's very kind."

He shrugged. "He's old, alone, and not well. We can't ignore that. I'd go clear his yard, we'd help him do some repairs, but he refuses."

He slid his arm around me, turning me around. "Enough about grumpy neighbor. I want to talk about my favorite subject."

"Which is?"

"You."

I scoffed. "Then you'll be bored since you saw me about eight hours ago, and since then I showered, took Lucy to school, and worked until Ronan showed up."

"How did you get the afternoon off?"

"I just signed off. I'm hourly, so it tracks my log-ins."

A note of worry crept into his voice. "So, you won't get paid?"

"We'll survive without a few hours' wages, Liam."

He made a displeased noise in the back of his throat but didn't say anything else about it.

"How did you become an insurance claims adjuster?"

"When I was pregnant with Lucy and Alan walked out, I had to support us. Another woman I knew told me she had been hired and liked it. They provided the training, you could work from home, and she knew they were looking. I applied and got the job." I smiled ruefully. "It's not the best-paying job, but I'm home for Lucy, which, when she was born, was the most important thing. I didn't want to dip into the settlement from Alan for child-care. I put that money in the bank for Lucy's education. I knew I wouldn't be able to afford to send her to university."

"You haven't touched it?" he asked. "I'm impressed."

"Don't be. I have had to dip into it when things were tough. If it weren't for Beth, I would have used way more of it. But Lucy can still go to university. I make sure she has everything she needs. I don't use a penny of it for myself. I don't want his money."

"Selfless," he muttered.

"No. It's my pride. I know that. But he didn't look after me when we were married, so he doesn't get to now either. The money is for Lucy."

He tightened his hand around mine. "Got it."

"No more talk of my ex, please. I don't want to think about him in this beautiful setting." I stopped and looked over the water, the sunlight shimmering on the surface. "It's so beautiful here. How do you tear yourself away and come into Toronto?"

"I know something equally beautiful and captivating there."

I met his eyes. He was staring straight at me, not the lovely view in front of us. I opened my mouth to brush off his words, then stopped. His gaze was focused, and his words ran true. It was how he really felt. Brushing off his compliments hurt him.

"Thank you," I whispered.

He swept me into his arms, kissing me with utter abandon. "That's my girl," he praised.

We sat on the porch, enjoying the breeze and the sun. I had grabbed some cookies from the freezer at home, and Liam munched on them as he sipped coffee and relaxed.

"I could get used to this," he muttered.

"You don't sit on the porch much?"

"I meant having you here. Stealing the occasional afternoon off work and spending it just enjoying the day." He sighed. "I rarely do that."

"You can kidnap me anytime," I teased.

"I might do that on a permanent basis," he said.

My cup froze partway to my mouth. "Liam," I admonished. "It's a little soon for that."

"Says who? Society?"

"Your family would think you've taken leave of your senses."

"Or come to them."

I set down my coffee. "Liam—"

He cut me off. "I'm not saying tomorrow. I'm thinking about the future."

"Lucy…" I trailed off when he held up his hand.

"Great day care here. And schools. You can do your job from anywhere, you told me. I'd add a desk in my office." He paused. "If you wanted to work. You wouldn't have to."

"Yes, I would. I never want to be in the position of not being able to take care of myself."

He was silent for a moment. "Whatever you want. I would never take away your right to make decisions."

I heard a trace of hurt in his voice, and I knew he was trying to assure me that he would take care of me. Of us.

He sat back. "A discussion for another time, maybe."

I nodded, picking up my coffee cup. I found it hard to swallow, though. So many words burned in my throat. Questions. Why was he so sure about us? The future? I had a feeling he was leaps and bounds ahead of me in his plans. A thought occurred to me, and I blurted out the words before I could think.

"What about kids?"

"What about them?" He leaned forward, resting his elbows on his thighs. "Do you want more kids?"

I hesitated. "I don't know."

"Why? You're such a great mother."

"Alan always said it was something I did that caused Lucy's deformity."

"We've established that Alan is an idiotic, narcissistic asshole whose opinion isn't worth the effort it takes for him to spew it."

"What if..." I swallowed. "What if he was right? What if I had another baby with—"

He cut me off. "It is unknown what causes a limb deformity. If it happened, then we would love him or her as much as Lucy is loved. This time, you would have backup, Paige. Me. My family. You wouldn't be alone. You won't have to face a pregnancy or anything alone. Ever again."

I glanced away, tears filling my eyes. Why did this man make me cry so much? He allowed me to express my thoughts and feelings, never judging.

"It scares me," I admitted.

He covered his hand with mine. "Hey, I didn't mean to get so serious. But I want you to know what I'm thinking about the future. You and Lucy are part of it. I would like more kids, and I want them with you."

I had to ask the question. "What if-what if I didn't—what if I couldn't?"

"Then the three of us would be a family."

"You would be satisfied with that?"

"I would never do anything that made you uncomfortable. I would never force you into a decision that caused you months of stress and worry."

"That's a big sacrifice."

"Having you in my life wouldn't make it a sacrifice. You're who I want. Lucy is a bonus. Anything else would be a gift."

I wanted to argue with him. He might resent me. I might resent myself if I got pregnant and it happened again. Lucy was amazing and did so well, but not every child would be the same.

His low *"uh oh"* interrupted my musings. I looked up to see his sister, Ava, walking up the driveway.

"I heard you had company," she said, sitting on the steps.

"And yet, here you are," Liam stated dryly, looking over at me with a wink.

Ava wasn't at all put out. She tossed her hair. "I just wanted to let you know Ronan says everything is in place. Your schedule is clear for Thursday."

"Great."

I assumed they were talking about a work project.

"And Dad wanted me to remind you it's your turn at the charity dinner. Saturday night."

"Oh God," Liam groaned. "I'll give you a thousand bucks to take my place."

She snorted. "Nope. I did it last time it was your turn. Mom and Dad will be there, so you're not alone. I listed you for a plus-one." Her gaze strayed to me. "If you need a sitter, I'd be happy to look after Lucy. You could bring her here, and we could have a girls' night."

"Sorry?" I asked, confused.

"We all have to attend various charity dinners. I hate them. Sitting listening to speeches, watching people with too much money who give to a cause only because so-and-so is also doing it," Liam explained.

"You don't do that?" I asked.

"No. We support the causes we believe in. We live it. This is one of them, but I still hate the dinners," he admitted. "Can I beg you to come with me?"

"Gee, you made it sound so great and all. How can I resist?" I teased.

He and Ava laughed. They looked very similar, with their heads tilted back and their dark hair glinting in the sun. They sounded alike as well. My imagination suddenly conjured up the same image, but this time, it was Liam laughing with a child. Our child. The baby sat on his knee, and the two of them were laughing, looking so alike my heart ached.

I suddenly wondered if maybe Liam was right. Maybe it would be worth the risk. Maybe I could give him everything he wanted.

I realized they were looking at me expectantly. "Um, sure, I'll go. I'll need to get a dress."

Ava shook her head. "Gah, don't. Mom will have something she's done in her shop. She's always making up samples and squirreling them away." She stood. "We can go see her now."

"Oh, um…"

Liam stood. "Good idea. You do that, I'll finish the garden plan, and we'll have the rest of the time together once you come back." He looked at Ava meaningfully. "Alone."

She rolled her eyes. "Whatever."

Cami was sitting on her deck as we approached. She stood, looking pleased. She hugged Ava, then me.

"Paige, how lovely to see you again."

"Thanks, Mrs.—uh, Cami. Ronan brought me out as a surprise for Liam."

She chuckled. "Well, I'm certain that made his day."

"Mom, Paige is going to the dinner with Liam on Saturday."

"Oh, lovely."

"She needs a dress. I told her not to buy one."

Cami waved her hands. "No, no. I have so many in the studio." She tilted her head, studying me. "In fact, I think I know the perfect one." She hooked her arm with mine. "Let's go peek."

We walked upstairs to the third floor. "This was our master suite," Cami explained. "Once the children were grown, Aiden had it converted so I could work here. We moved to the second floor and made two bedrooms into our room since we no longer needed five bedrooms for the kids." She lifted one shoulder as she opened the door to her studio. "The house is still too big for only us, but we love it."

The space was bright with the skylights and big windows. It held a small desk, some fabric swatches, and a large sewing table with three different machines. A little dais was in the center of the room. Along the back wall were floor-to-ceiling doors. I knew she was a successful, exclusive designer, but the room seemed too small. At my curious look, Cami explained.

"My main studio is in Toronto. But I don't work as much now, so this is perfect. I mostly do dresses for family. I have two very capable women at the studio in Toronto who do the sewing." She held up her hands. "Arthritis makes sewing difficult at times. I design, and my ladies sew."

"I don't want to cause you any trouble."

"Nonsense." She clapped her hands. "Let's see what I have." She opened one of the closet doors, pursing her lips. "It's only semi-formal, thank goodness. I hate long gowns in the summer," she said as she shifted through jewel-toned material. "I was thinking the yellow, but maybe, ah—yes! The blue."

She pulled out a dress, and my breath hitched. Rich, royal-blue fabric caught the light, the subtle beading along the bodice glinting. "This would suit your figure, and the color would look lovely with your skin." She handed it to me. "There's a privacy screen over there. Slip it on and let me see."

My hands shook as I slid it off the hanger. I had never worn anything so lovely. The dress was smooth and whisper-soft. I slipped it on and came out from behind the screen. "It's a little tight in the top," I said, feeling disappointed.

"I can let out the seams a bit. Come stand here." Cami pointed to the raised platform, and I stepped onto it. She walked around me, nodding and muttering. "Lift the shoulders, adjust the bodice, take up the hem an inch, maybe two."

Before I could protest about the work, she stepped closer and began to pin the fabric. "Blue is Liam's favorite color. He will love this."

"It needs too much work. Your hands——"

Cami cut me off with a laugh. "This is easy. Simple seams." She showed me the inside of the dress. "These are basted. I always only baste the sides since I don't know which of my girls will need a dress. I can let it out a little here, but once I adjust the shoulders, it won't need much." She spun me around. "Look."

I gasped as I looked at myself in the dress. The blue fabric hugged my breasts and flared out at my waistline. Pinned up, it ended just below my knees, showing off my legs. The material draped and molded itself to me, glowing in the light. The added chiffon formed a square neckline and showed off my full breasts to their advantage. The sleeves were artfully draped, barely covering the top of my arms.

"Is this silk?" I asked, fingering the fabric of the full skirt.

"Yes."

"It's so gorgeous."

Cami smiled. "Thank you. It suits you. You have lovely shoulders and arms." She pursed her lips. "You'll need a strapless bra."

"Okay."

She twisted my hair. "Wear your hair up to show off the neckline. A pair of long earrings, nothing too over the top. No other jewelry unless you want to wear a bracelet. Let the dress shine."

I could only nod, unable to take my eyes off my reflection. "I have never worn anything so beautiful."

Ava came over, carrying a pair of strappy shoes. "These, Mom?"

Cami nodded. "Yes. Slip those on, Paige dear."

I did as she asked, shocked at how the heels changed my posture. Ava held out her hand. "What about these?"

"Yes, excellent choice." Cami handed me a pair of simple drop earrings with tiny blue and white stones that caught the light in a burst of brilliance. "Try these."

I paused. "They, ah, aren't real, are they?"

Cami laughed. "No. Crystals. I keep a bunch of accessories we use for special occasions. No need in wasting money buying something you might only use once."

She met my surprised gaze in the mirror and shrugged. "Growing up, my sister and I lived together and only had each other. We had to scrimp and save every penny, and we shared all sorts of things. Emmy was part of that. Some habits you never break. Why spend money on something you'll wear on only one occasion and then tuck it in a drawer and forget it? If Dee needs something, she borrows it. So does Emmy. All the girls. If they buy something new, they add it to the collection." She grinned. "Our own little shop."

"And the shoes?" I asked.

Cami laughed. "My obsession, I admit. Ava and I wear the same size, and I thought you looked about a seven as well. Same thing. Why go buy a pair you might never wear again? Borrow these for the night."

"You are too generous."

"Nonsense. You mean a great deal to my son, so that means you're family. And that is what we do. We're there for family."

"Thank you," I whispered, my throat thick.

"I'm bringing Lucy here for a girls' night on Saturday. We're going to have a sleepover at my place," Ava said, sounding excited.

Cami clapped her hands in delight. "Then we can have brunch on Sunday. You can enjoy a lie-in with Liam and come to the house around eleven."

My cheeks colored at her words. She assumed I would be coming home with Liam and sleeping over. Which meant she also assumed we had—

She laughed at my blush. "I'm not a regular mother. I'm quite aware my children are adults and act as such. I remember Aiden and I when we were younger. We couldn't keep our hands off each other."

Ava laughed as she sat down. "You still can't. It's disgusting, Mom. I keep telling you that." But she met my eyes and winked.

Cami stepped back with a smile. "You change, and we'll have tea and visit for a bit. I'll work on the dress tomorrow, and you'll look beautiful on Saturday."

I slipped off the dress and followed Cami and Ava back downstairs. While Cami was making tea, I looked around the house Liam had grown up in. It was spacious and open. Lots of wood, with a huge double-sided, stone fireplace in the middle that separated the kitchen/dining room from the living room. Family pictures were everywhere, soft scatter rugs on top of gleaming oak floors. Heavy furniture, including a massive dining table. I could picture Ava, Liam, and the triplets around the table with Cami and Aiden, all talking and laughing, the noise level no doubt high. The front windows overlooked the water and beach below.

Ava stood beside me at the windows. "I always loved this view," she said.

"What a wonderful place to grow up," I murmured.

"It was. I love it here. We all do. Even those of us who don't choose to live here full time come back every chance they get. It's special."

"Was it fun being the only girl in the house, or did the boys torment you?"

She laughed. "Both. They loved to tease and play tricks. But if anyone else got in my face, they became my fiercest protectors. My dad made sure he taught me the same moves as the boys, so I could defend myself as well. In fact, he enrolled us all in karate. I was the only one who kept at it. I have a black belt."

"Wow. Impressive."

She waggled her eyebrows, looking mischievous. "Keeps the boys in line. They know if they step off it, I'll flip them."

"You can flip Liam?"

"Easy. It's not the size of your opponent. It's how you use your own strength. I'll show you if you like."

I had to laugh. "I'd love to see that."

"Done."

CHAPTER NINE
PAIGE

Cami called to us, and we sat down, sipping the fragrant tea. She turned to me.

"From what I understand, you have no family?"

"No. My parents are gone, and I have no siblings. No uncles, aunts, anything. It's only Lucy and me. Plus, Beth and Evan, of course."

Cami beamed at me. Her smile lit up her face, and I could understand why Aiden called her his Sunshine. She glowed when she smiled. "I adore Beth and Evan. And your Lucy is a little doll. We are so happy for Ronan and Liam." She laughed. "All my boys have fallen in love so quickly and close together." She glanced at Ava. "I wonder what is next?"

Ava rolled her eyes. "Not me, Mom. I'm far too busy with work."

"Never say never."

Ava laughed. "Don't hold your breath."

Cami smiled affectionately. "I want you to have what your father and I have. I want that for all my children."

"Four out of five is pretty good. Soon, you'll be bouncing grand-kids on your knee, and you'll be too busy to worry about me." Ava nudged me. "Get on that, would you? Help a girl out."

I felt the color drain from my face, and Ava looked horrified.

"Oh my God, I'm sorry. I shouldn't have said that. I mean, maybe you can't or——" she dropped her head into her hands "——oh God, I'm sorry."

"It's okay," I assured her. "It's just…"

"Just?" Cami prompted.

I had no idea why I spoke up. "I know Liam wants children. I'm worried about having another baby," I admitted.

"Because of Lucy?" Cami asked quietly.

"Yes."

"Then you can be a family of three."

"Is that fair to your son?"

She paused. "I don't think my son fell in love with you for your uterus, Paige. He fell in love with your heart. Your spirit. Your mind. He would love Lucy as his own." She pursed her lips. "Do you recall meeting Van and his wife Liv on the weekend?"

"Yes. They had a lovely family."

She smiled. "Not one of those children is Van's biological offspring. He met Liv when Sammy was five and adopted her when they got married. They adopted Reed and Mila together.

You would never know that. He loves them fiercely." She patted my hand. "Family isn't only about blood. It's about love."

She sipped her tea, letting me digest her words. "Five children or one child. You're still a family. Don't let your fears of a what-if that might never happen stop you from being happy. If my son tells you he is content with only Lucy, you should believe him."

"I don't want him to regret me. Regret us."

Cami laughed. "The only thing he would regret is losing you. I know Liam. I know his heart. He is much like Aiden. Like all my family. When they love, it is with an abiding passion and strength that will change your life. Never doubt that."

I blinked. "I'm sorry. I shouldn't have said anything."

She shook her head. "No, I'm glad you did. Maybe knowing about Van will help you."

"It does, I think."

"Good."

The door opened, and Liam walked in.

"There you are."

I laughed. "You knew I was here."

He looked at his watch. "It's a dress. One dress. You've been gone over an hour."

Cami stood. "We were having tea." She laid a hand on his arm and leaned up to kiss his cheek. He bent to make it easier for her to reach. "Stop being so impatient."

"I don't get her alone enough."

She patted his arm and met my gaze. "Told you," it said.

"Sit down and have tea, then you can take her home. I'll try to stop your father from coming for a visit later."

Liam sat beside me with a groan. "If he knows she's here, he'll invent an excuse."

Cami handed him a mug. "Then I guess I'll have to keep him busy."

I laughed at the uncomfortable look on his and Ava's faces. Cami might be quite relaxed about her kids' sex lives, but they had no desire to know about their parents' activities. Cami was well aware of that fact, and she met my eyes with a wide grin. I winked at her, and she chuckled.

Liam cleared his throat. "Did you find something to wear?"

"Yes," I responded. "It's so lovely," I gushed. "I've never worn anything so beautiful."

"My mom is pretty amazing," he said, sounding proud.

"Your whole family is."

He leaned close, his mouth brushing my earlobe. "They're yours now too—if you want them."

I met his eyes. Warm, open, and filled with love.

I squeezed his hand in response, unable to talk. He affected me so deeply, I couldn't find the words. I had never felt this way about a man. Liam filled me with emotion with his honesty and lack of guile. Something he had obviously inherited from his mother. She was a straight shooter.

He seemed to realize I was overwhelmed and turned to his mother, asking a question about the weekend. I sipped my tea, listening to them chat, wondering if there would come a day I would feel as if I fit in. As if I were part of this wonderful family.

A huge part of me yearned for it.

I needed the rest of me to catch up.

LIAM

Paige was quiet as we walked toward the house. She seemed a little withdrawn, and I wondered if today had been too much. I knew Sunday with my family had overwhelmed her. Then talking about her past and ex. Her confession today about having another baby surprised me, but I supposed it was only natural. After she'd left with Ava, I had a hard time concentrating on the garden plan. I had to admit I was somewhat disappointed. I had always wanted a large family like my own. But if Paige didn't want that, I knew I owed it to her to make sure I would be happy with only the three of us. No matter how I looked at it, I came to the same conclusion. I would rather have Paige and Lucy than someone else and babies. I never expected to fall in love so quickly. I always thought I would meet someone, date, and eventually fall for them. But with Paige, it was hard and fast. She dominated my thoughts in the day. Slipped into my dreams at night if I wasn't with her. My desire for her was constant. And I knew, without a doubt, my feelings would only grow stronger.

I glanced down at her, noticing the small vee between her eyes which indicated she was thinking too hard about something. Worried.

I pulled her to the chair beside me once we climbed the steps.

"What's going on in that pretty head of yours, Sweet Pea?"

"Your mother says you didn't fall in love with me for my uterus."

I lifted my eyebrows in surprise. "Well, I'm not sure how that topic came up, but she's right. The first time I saw you, 'Wow, I bet she has an amazing uterus,' wasn't what crossed my mind. Pretty sure your spectacular rack made the first impression."

That made her laugh, and her shoulders lost some of their tension. She told me what Ava had said and her reaction.

"I didn't plan on talking about it with your mother and sister. It just came out."

"I never thought to mention Van. His kids are simply that—his kids. My cousins, for lack of a better term." I took her hands in mine. "Paige, there's no rush. We don't even have to talk about this again until you're ready. And if you never are, then we'll figure out our next step. You are what is important to me. You and Lucy. Getting to know each other now. Enjoying life together now." I met her eyes. "I've never tried to get someone pregnant. For all I know, I'm shooting blanks. Would you love me less because of that?"

"No."

"Then relax. Let's enjoy now, and let the future take care of itself. Can we put it aside and enjoy this evening?"

She smiled and cupped my cheek. "Yes."

"Good. I am starving, and that pot roast smells like heaven. Feed me. Please."

She stood and went into the house. I followed her, ogling her ass. I always liked her ass.

"You know, I think the first day I met you, your ass might have appealed as much as your breasts. Both left an impression," I mused out loud. "I do remember wanting to grope them equally."

She burst out laughing. "Such a way with words, Liam."

I shrugged with a grin. "It's a gift."

She muttered something about *incorrigible Callaghans.*

I kissed her neck as I reached around her to grab some plates.

"You like me incorrigible."

She rolled her eyes, but she didn't deny it.

I switched off the TV and tossed the remote on the table. It had been a great evening. Paige was relaxed and happy. After a delicious dinner, we took another walk on the beach. We waved at Bentley and Emmy, spoke with Nan and Pops, who were out for their nightly stroll, and studiously ignored the dim light coming from my parents' bedroom as we walked past their house. I just couldn't think about that. Ronan was in Toronto with Beth, and we called and talked to Lucy, who informed us she was having fun and that wings were now her favorite food. Mr. Teddy apparently thought so as well.

"Momma, Mr. Teddy needs a bath. He went headfirst in the sauce."

Paige laughed, her voice patient. "I'll give him one tomorrow."

"Otay."

I knew Paige felt better once she talked to Lucy. She told me she wasn't worried but felt odd.

"I've never been away from her for the night. Not once."

"We can head in. I'll sleep there," I offered.

"No. She's fine, and Beth will call me. It's just…new."

I slipped my arms around her and hugged her. She held me tight.

"I'll have you home before she wakes up."

"Thank you."

I kissed her. "Anytime."

I glanced over at her. She had drifted during the movie, leaning against me, snuggled into my side. "You want to go to bed?" I asked.

"No, it's too early."

"How about a bath?"

Her eyes lit up. "In that huge tub?"

"You have to share."

She waggled her eyebrows. "I was planning on it."

I held out my hand, and she took it. "I'll lock up. You go start it filling. It takes a while."

I made my rounds, checking the doors and windows. It was something I always did. Our houses were safe, the compound gate locked and the crime rate here next to nothing, but my dad had always "made the rounds" and checked to make sure his family was safe, and I did the same thing.

I heard the water running and headed to my room. I pulled off my Henley and undid my jeans as I sauntered over to the bathroom door. Paige was topless in front of the mirror, pinning up her hair. Her pretty neck was on display. She'd told me what my mom had said about her shoulders, and I realized she was right. They were lovely. Smooth and round, her collarbone clearly defined and the elegant arch to her chin—she was gorgeous. Her arms were toned as she lifted them, the movement causing her breasts to sway. I crossed the room, standing behind her. She watched as I lit a couple of candles I had placed on the vanity earlier and flicked off the overhead light. I pressed a kiss to her shoulder, sliding my hands to the front and cupping her, slowly letting my fingers tease her nipples.

"Yeah," I murmured. "These definitely got my attention first. I wanted you to climb me like a tree and let me play with them while you did." I moved my mouth to the juncture where her neck met her shoulder, trailing my tongue over her skin.

She shivered.

"Cold, baby?"

"No," she whispered breathlessly.

I rolled her nipples, never breaking eye contact in the mirror. The candlelight was a dim glow in the room, but her eyes were on fire. The desire in them matched my own and made it rage even higher. She arched her back, pushing her breasts fully into my hands. She whimpered as I increased the pressure of my fingers, her nipples now hard, tight peaks under my touch.

"I love how responsive you are," I murmured against her skin, finding the sensitive area behind her ear and nuzzling it.

"Liam," she sighed.

I slid my hands down her torso, flicking open the buttons on her pants and slipping my hands inside. I pushed down the material, taking her lacy underwear with it. Her pants fell to the floor with a low whoosh. I cupped her possessively, feeling the heat between her legs. "You gonna get in that bath with me, Paige?"

"Yes."

"You gonna let me fuck you in that big tub? Ride me like a stallion with my cock deep inside you?"

"Oh God," she moaned quietly.

"No. Me." I kissed her neck again. "I want to hear you tonight. It's just us. No kids, no Beth. Just us. I want to hear you scream my name. Moan. Beg me for more. I want to know every little thought in your head as I fuck you fast and hard. Then I'm going to do it again, this time slowly. On my bed with your legs wrapped around me and my cock making you crazy." I bit down on her neck, soothing the nip with my tongue.

With a cry, she turned and flung her arms around my neck. Our mouths crashed together, our tongues sliding and tasting. I explored her mouth, certain I would never get enough of her taste. Of the feeling of having her in my arms. The deep sense of satisfaction I felt when I was buried inside her. She clawed at my neck, pulling me as close as she could. Her breasts pressed into my chest, the softness of her flesh yielding to my muscles. I lifted her in my arms and headed for the tub. I stepped in and lowered us into the warm water, never stopping in my possession of her mouth. She groaned as the water rose over us, the depth and length of the tub unparalleled. That was the reason I'd bought it. The room, the high placement of the overflow. I could sink in and float if I wanted to. And with Paige in there with me, it was perfect.

I sat up, Paige wrapped around me. Our mouths moved in a frenzy. I had my hands all over her, touching and caressing. Her arms and shoulders, her back and spine, cupping her full ass. I licked my way down her neck, sucking her nipples as she gripped the sides of the tub, groaning and pleading, her back arched and her head thrown back. My cock was wedged between us, hard and aching.

"I can't hear you," I growled. "Tell me what you want."

She surprised me when she pushed away, breaking our contact. She wrapped her hand around my cock, pumping it, then slid her hands under my ass, pulling at me. "Up," she demanded.

I lifted my hips, shouting in pleasure as she lowered her head, licking at me. The heat of her mouth engulfed me, and I cursed. She worked me with her hand and mouth, circling the tip, tonguing my shaft, sucking and pumping. I had never seen a sight as erotic as her kneeling in the hot water, her lips wrapped around me. It was my turn to grip the sides of the tub as she sped up, her wicked mouth and tongue doing things to my cock that should be illegal. I felt the tightening in my balls, and I groaned.

"Stop, baby. You need to stop. I want to be inside you."

She lifted her head, pulling back slowly, dropping a final kiss to my crown. She rose up, the water sluicing off her skin, the steam rolling off her body. I reached forward, dragging her back to my lap and kissing her. She tasted of me, the sharp tang of her mouth making me groan. I grabbed her hips, and she shifted, rising over me. Our eyes locked as she positioned me and slowly sat down, my cock sliding in inch by inch, the heat of the water replaced by a different, slicker wet. I let my head fall back as ripples of pleasure shook me.

Paige groaned. "You feel so good inside me, Liam."

I flexed my hips, sinking deeper until we were flush. Paige tightened her inner muscles, squeezing all around me. She met my gaze, a smile on her lips. "You promised me a good fucking, Liam. You gonna live up to that?"

I sat up, gripping her neck with one hand, anchoring her to me with the other hand on her hip. I began to move, not holding back. I slammed into her, grunting and groaning. She held on to the tub's edge, meeting my thrusts and giving me exactly what I asked for. She pleaded and begged. Clawed at my back, arched her neck, and rode me. Cried out my name. Water splashed over the sides, hitting the floor like small explosions. And still, we moved. I licked and bit her nipples. She scraped her nails over mine, making me hiss in pleasure. She orgasmed, her eyes wide, her groans loud as I rode it out, her muscles clamping down on me.

"I'm not finished," I demanded. "You're going to give me another one."

She mewled, clutching my shoulders. She buried her face into my neck as I grabbed her hips, moving hard and fast. Shudders raced through her, and she cried out again as my release crashed through me, hot and bright. I wrapped her in my arms as I lost myself to the sensations coursing through my body, finally stilling in the steam-filled room, the water settling, the quiet of the evening a balm to our ragged breathing.

Carefully, I lay back, taking her with me. I used my foot to turn the water back on, letting the tub fill again. We'd lost a lot of water. I glanced over the side with a chuckle. "Good thing I added a floor drain."

Lazily, Paige peeked over the edge. "Wow. Lake Liam."

She settled against my chest, and I stroked her hair that had come loose, the ends trailing in the water.

"I like this tub," she whispered.

"I like you."

"I liked you fucking me in this tub."

I grinned against her head. "You're going to love what I do to you in my bed, then."

She giggled, lifting her head. "Not sure if I can move right now."

I kissed her, my mouth lingering on her softness. "I'm not in a hurry. We have all night. We can soak for a while."

She burrowed closer. "Good."

CHAPTER TEN
PAIGE

I snuggled closer to Liam, his body shifting to align with mine. He loved to be close when sleeping. If I shifted, so did he. When I rolled, he followed. I had to admit, I loved it. I opened my eyes, studying his face as he slumbered. He looked younger than his thirty-three years in repose. His skin was smooth, his body relaxed. He made the occasional face, pursing his lips as if tasting something, and every so often a small snore escaped.

After we had climbed out of the tub and dried off, we slid under the softest sheets I'd ever felt. He pulled me to his chest, the flicker of the candles reflecting in the bathroom mirror the only light.

"Tell me about growing up here," I asked. I wanted to hear his voice, listen to his stories. We'd talked enough about me and my past. I wanted to hear something light. Joyful.

Liam chuckled and shared some funny moments from when he was young. Adventures he and his brothers had. The times he got into trouble. The way they teased Ava mercilessly.

"Once when I was about seven or eight, the triplets and I were climbing on the rocks in the cove I showed you today," he recalled. "We were specifically told not to play there. It was dangerous—which made it that much more inviting." He chuckled. "We were playing pirates, I think, and Paul slipped and got his foot caught between some rocks. We tried and couldn't get it out, so Ronan went home and came back with a bottle of olive oil. He figured if we made Paul's skin slippery enough, we could get it out, and our parents would be none the wiser."

"Makes sense."

"Unless there was water all around the rocks and an entire bottle of olive oil made no difference. Then Jeremy got it in his head that a wave might come in and be so big it would drown Paul, and he started to freak out. He ran screaming before I could stop him, and of course, that brought all the 'rents to the cove."

"Uh oh," I giggled. "How'd you get Paul's foot out?"

Liam shifted, his chest shaking with laughter. "My dad just lifted the damn rock. But getting caught in the rocks wasn't the big thing. The bottle of olive oil Ronan grabbed was from a little town in Italy. My dad had given it to my mom as a gift. It was some exclusive, rare pressing and was expensive as hell. She only used it for special dishes. And we had just poured it into the water."

I joined in his laughter. "What happened?"

"We had to do extra chores until we paid for the olive oil. And we had to go to bed after supper for a week with no dessert. That was the worst part."

I stroked his face. "Poor baby. You were probably starved."

"My dad still laughs about it, but my mom gets downright irate when he does. She liked that olive oil."

I hummed. "Good olive oil is a wonderful thing."

"Maddox and Dee bought her a different bottle when they went to Italy a few years later. She kept it in the cupboard with a lock."

I snickered in amusement.

"Your mom and Ava were outnumbered all the time."

"They hold their own," he stated dryly. "I know not to mess with them. My back still hasn't recovered from the last skirmish with Ava."

"How long ago was that?"

"About nine years."

I lifted my head. "What happened?"

He groaned. "I was teasing her. She's pretty jumpy sometimes, and I scared her as she walked around the corner. She got pissed and told me off, which made me laugh. She's half my size, so I wasn't worried." He met my eyes. "I forgot about the black belt. I did it again the next day, and before I could blink, she had flipped me. One moment, I was standing. The next, I was flat on my back on the floor, blinking up at the ceiling, wondering how a truck had gotten into the Hub and hit me."

I tried to hold back my laughter and failed. "I guess you don't hide around corners anymore, do you?"

"Nope."

I kept my head down, the laughter bubbling up. Suddenly I found myself pinned under a growling Liam. "You think that's funny, Sweet Pea?"

"No," I lied.

"How do you like being flipped? Trapped under me?" He ran his hands up my arms, lifting them over my head. "At my mercy?" he rasped, holding my wrists with one large hand and feathering the other over my skin, making me shiver. He lowered his head to my neck and kissed it, swirling his tongue on

my skin. "I think I promised you a long, slow lovemaking session," he breathed into my ear. "And I think you're about to get it."

I tugged on my arms, and he released his grip, letting me wrap them around his neck. "I do love a man who keeps his promises."

His mouth covered mine, and I was lost.

I blinked, realizing I had been reliving last night. I glanced up and met Liam's sleepy gaze. His hazel eyes were soft, his voice low as he kissed me.

"I could get used to waking up with you tucked against me."

"Lucy would be in here driving you crazy."

He smiled, his eyes crinkling in the corners. "My little munchkin. I guess I'll have to wear sleep pants."

"Unless you want a lot of personal questions in the mornings, yes."

He kissed me again. "I look forward to it." He glanced at the clock. "Speaking of which, I need to get you home."

Part of me hated the fact that I had to get out of this comfortable bed. Leave Liam's arms and face the day. But I also knew Lucy would be awake soon, and I needed to be there. I sat up and yawned. "Okay, Mr. Callaghan. Take me home."

Ronan was sitting on the steps as we pulled up, a steaming cup of coffee in his hand. He smiled at me as I got to the steps.

"How was your night, kids?"

I laughed. "Good. Yours?"

"Awesome. We built a pretty cool Lego house, watched *Finding Nemo*—twice—and ate popcorn. Lucy fell asleep on me, Evan passed out on the sofa, and Beth said we were all snoring."

"Wow, you know how to party."

He took a sip of coffee, suddenly serious. "I wanted to take everyone's mind off all the shit. I think it worked." He nodded at Liam, who came up behind me, resting his hand on my hip.

"You ready for tomorrow?"

"Yep."

"Good."

"You guys have a big project tomorrow or something?"

Ronan nodded. "Something."

I patted his shoulder as I went past. "Good luck with it."

Inside, I peeked at Lucy. She was still asleep, but her feet were moving. That was always a sign she'd be awake soon.

I hurried to my room and changed, and then I headed to the kitchen, mixing up some "pandcake" batter. A few moments later, I heard the thumps of little feet, and I turned, bending down and holding out my arms.

"Morning, Lucy-loo!"

She flung herself into my embrace, and I sat down, listening to her recount of the night before. I didn't think she had missed me at all until she squeezed my neck. "I wished you was there!"

I smiled.

"Did you have fun on your date?"

"My date?"

She nodded. "Ronan said you was on a date wif Liam." She leaned close. "Did he kiss you, Momma?"

"Kiss me?" I repeated again.

She nodded. "You hafta kiss on a date."

"Oh, we kissed, all right," Liam said, striding in. "I kissed your momma every chance I got. Even when I had to chase her."

Lucy laughed in delight as Liam took her from me, pretending she was an airplane and flying her around the room. He settled her against his chest and listened as she lectured him on something. He nodded, looking serious, and assured her he had done exactly that. "It was just pretend."

"Otay."

"Go get dressed, baby. Breakfast will be ready soon," I said.

She glanced up at Liam. "You stay? Momma makes good pandcakes."

"As if I could resist," he teased and watched her hurry down the hall.

I tested the pan and poured the first batter onto the hot griddle. "What was that about?" I asked.

He sighed and leaned against the counter. "Um, I am supposed to get permission before I touch you. There are private parts no one is allowed near. Chasing does not indicate consent." He scrubbed his face. "I have a lot to learn. And, no, she didn't say it exactly like that, but I got the gist."

He hung his head. "And apparently I've been touching a lot of no-no places on you."

I sidled up to him and kissed his cheek. "You're doing great. It's something they teach at school now. And you can touch my no-no places anytime you want."

His smile could light up the room. "Excellent."

Thursday morning, Beth left to meet Evan's teacher, and a short while later, Liam called and told me what the project they had been working on entailed. It had nothing to do with business and everything to do with Evan. He explained that BAM and ABC were going to Evan's school to talk about bullying. Ronan had arranged all of it.

"I didn't want to say anything in case something fell through. The principal has no idea what we're doing. Mr. Humphries arranged it all with Ronan and Bentley." He paused. "Could you come to the school? I know Beth is going to be shocked. I'm sure she'd love you there."

"Absolutely."

"I'll swing by and pick you up on my way. Fifteen minutes enough time?"

"Yes."

At the school, I found Beth and Evan at the back of the full auditorium. Ronan called Evan up to the front, and we watched as he slowly made his way to join them and listened to the way Ronan introduced him. There was no doubt of their connection after his words.

Watching all the men and women of these companies, this family, speak about what they did, their beliefs, and their experiences was riveting. Aiden was hilarious when he cursed mildly and his family all chuckled, but his words hit home with the kids. Beth held my hand tightly as she watched these people rally around her brother. Show the school he hadn't been lying when he said he knew the men of BAM. That he meant something special to them. Ronan stood behind him, his large hands resting on Evan's shoulders, and more than once, Beth choked back a sob. I saw the principal staring her way.

"I think someone is going to eat humble pie," I whispered to her.

"He can wait," she replied.

Liam was on the other side of Ronan and, a couple of times, leaned down to listen to something Evan would say. He ruffled his hair at one point, making Evan laugh. He looked toward the back of the auditorium as if searching for me. I waggled my fingers, not sure if he could see me, but I saw his waggle back so I knew he could. He looked every inch a businessman in a suit and tie. The jacket stretched across his shoulders and the pants fit his thick legs so well, I knew the suit had to be custom tailored for him. His hair brushed the back of the collar. He was devastatingly sexy, and his outfit was vastly different from what he usually wore. I approved.

The Q&A was long, but no one was impatient. There was no glancing at wrists or rushed responses. When Bentley wrapped it up and announced the help line, the affection I had been feeling for Liam's family exploded into love. What an incredible group of human beings. I understood now what Liam had said about the charities they believed in.

"We support the causes we believe in. We live it."

Afterward, they all gathered around Evan and Beth. A circle of support. Beth looked at them with tears in her eyes. "Thank you. For what you did for Evan, thank you."

Liam huffed. "We couldn't let them get away with calling him a liar."

"Or hurting him," Aiden added, his hand on Evan's shoulder. "Not happening again."

"The help line was very generous," I said.

Bentley smiled. "We sponsor a lot of help lines and programs. We do it for Aiden and kids like him. So they know they aren't as alone as it seems."

"Do you think it will make a difference?" Beth asked quietly to Ronan.

He grinned. "All the firepower of BAM and ABC claiming Evan as one of ours? Absolutely. I think the little fuckers will think twice about bullying anyone."

"Ronan," Bentley hissed. "We're in a school, for heaven's sake. With kids. Watch the language."

"If my dad can do it, so can I," he protested. "Besides, there're no kids around."

"Evan is here," Beth pointed out dryly.

"Evan isn't a kid. He's family," Ronan stated firmly. The rest of them nodded, and I saw Beth's eyes fill with tears again.

Ronan leaned down, his voice quiet. "I'm taking Beth and Evan to lunch. Can I have her for the night? I called her boss, and he gave her the night off."

"Absolutely. We'll have a night together with Evan. You take care of her."

He winked. "I plan to."

Liam slipped his arm around my waist. "Any chance I can convince you to play hooky with me?"

"Already booked off."

"That's my girl."

Evan was a different boy that night. He sat and talked to Liam for a while as I bathed Lucy. He'd eaten all his dinner, laughed and teased Lucy, and insisted on helping with dishes. He told me he'd received a lot of attention at school after lunch, as he dried the dishes.

"Not the bad kind this time," he assured me.

"How do you feel about that?"

He shrugged. "I know who the real people are, Paige. The ones who liked me before this morning. I'm going to stick with them."

"You're a smart boy, Evan."

He smiled. "Ronan told me it would happen, and he was right. I'd already figured that."

We sat and watched *Finding Nemo* for the one-millionth time this week. Lucy was fixated on the little fish with the bad fin, and we went through bouts of watching it to excess. She insisted Liam had to see it since Ronan had watched it last night. Luckily, she fell asleep halfway through. Evan headed down the hall to do some homework, and I tucked Lucy into bed.

Liam was stretched out on the sofa when I got back, his feet hanging over the end. I smiled at him. "Tired?"

He held out his arms and tugged me on top of him. I settled on his chest, and he stroked up and down my back.

"I shouldn't be," he mused. "We had a good nap this afternoon."

"After we finished your little lesson," I muttered.

"I needed to figure out all the no-no places. Not my fault I kept forgetting. I needed to be sure."

"Well, you made sure, all right. Twice."

"Um, three times," he corrected. "You sort of slipped right into that last one pretty fast."

I slapped his chest. "You are no gentleman."

"I cleaned up pretty good today."

"Oh yeah," I agreed. "You were so sexy in your suit."

He looked pleased. "Oh yeah? You thought so?"

"How could I not? All the women were staring at you. You were so hot. You must know that."

He shrugged. "I'm okay. But I like to know my woman thinks I'm hot."

"I do. Smoking hot."

He shut his eyes. "Stop."

But he was smiling.

CHAPTER ELEVEN
LIAM

Saturday, I picked up Paige and Lucy around three. I hadn't seen Paige since I'd kissed her goodbye Friday morning before dawn had broken. I hated driving away and I hated not seeing her, but it had been a crazy day since I had pushed so much to the side all week. I had meetings late into the evening, and when I had called her, I could hear the exhaustion in her voice. It amazed me how much I missed her. How quickly she'd become vital to me. Her voice and her smile made my day. Touching her, feeling her mouth underneath mine, was addictive.

I was glad when she agreed to come out to Port Albany and get ready for the dinner here. Ava was excited, and she and Gracie had all sorts of plans for Lucy. Lucy was looking forward to seeing them, as well as Gracie's daughter. She was quite fascinated with Kylie and even brought her a gift of one of her favorite stuffed toys.

"Momma says it's good to share," she informed me when she showed it to me.

"It is," I agreed, ruffling her hair. "You are a great kid, Munchkin."

She huffed. "I knowed that."

I held back my grin.

Paige looked nervous when I picked her up, and I knew tonight was making her anxious. I took her hand in mine as we drove down the highway. "Tonight will be fun. Mom and Dad are looking forward to having you there. Bentley and Emmy will be there. So will Mad Dog and Dee. We have a whole table, so it'll be great."

"I've never been to one this fancy."

I shrugged. "They really are all the same. Lots of people, probably a bland catered meal, free bar, which means people will overindulge. A silent auction and lots of posturing." I winked. "Am I selling it?"

She laughed. "I can hardly wait."

"We have a good time. We mostly keep to ourselves. There are people we talk with, I always like to see what's on the auction table, and I overbid. It goes to the charity. BAM and ABC donate."

"What do you donate?"

"A weekend on the houseboat. A consult with Liv for design. Me for landscaping. Bentley often offers a trip to one of the properties the company owns."

Her eyes widen. "I guess I won't be bidding."

"There're lots of things. Last year, Mom bought a painting by one of the kids the charity helped. She loved it, and the kid was thrilled. Emmy bought a cake someone had made. There's often a huge range."

"Oh."

"The only constant is we usually eat pizza after we get home. Dad stops and picks it up on our way out of town. No matter the venue unless it's our winery, the food is usually flavorless, and the portions are minute."

"Rubber chicken?"

"Basically."

"I'll remember that. You make this date sound like so much fun, Liam," she said dryly.

I flashed a grin at her. "I'll be there."

"Then it's a great date."

"I figured." I pulled into the complex. "Let's drop the munchkin off and get ready." I winked at her. "We might even have time for a nap."

———

I tugged down my sleeves, the cuff links glinting in the light. I went all out tonight with a black suit, pure-white shirt, and a tie in royal blue my mom gave me to match Paige's dress. I trimmed my beard, made sure my hair was neat, and shoved my feet into shoes so shiny I was blinded by the glare. They were uncomfortable as hell, reminding me why I preferred to dress casually.

I walked into the living room, glancing at the closed door to the guest room. Paige had wanted to get ready in private and refused to use my room. I was anxious to see her, having caught a glimpse of the dress my mom had brought over. I had a feeling she was going to knock me off my feet.

I rolled my shoulders and stretched my neck. Our "nap" had done me good, and I was relaxed and ready to take my girl out and show her off. I made sure my credit card was in my pocket in case I saw her eyeing anything on the auction table. I wanted to spoil her.

A soft throat-clearing made me turn around, and I drank in the sight before me.

Paige was a goddess.

The rich blue silk swirled around her knees. Her sexy shoulders and collarbone were on display, the skin creamy and soft against the blue. Her hair was swept up, and her earrings sparkled under the light. Her legs, always firm and shapely, looked amazing in those heels. She wore more makeup than I was used to, her eyes smoky and sexy and her lips stained in a deep red.

She took my breath away.

I drew closer, shaking my head. "Paige, baby. I have no words. You are *stunning*. That dress. Those heels. Jesus, I'm going to have a hard time taking you out in public." I pressed a kiss to her forehead, inhaling her soft scent. "I don't want to share. I want to keep you here and ravish you."

She blushed, looking down. Then she smiled and met my eyes. "I like those words."

I lifted her hand and kissed it. "Good. I'll keep them coming all night."

"You aren't going to kiss me?"

"I don't want to mess up your, ah, mouth. The lipstick."

"It's non-smudgeable. Kiss-proof."

"Really?"

"That's what the ad says."

I stepped closer. "Frankly, that's like a challenge, then. I can't say no. I need to prove them wrong."

Her eyes danced. "Good."

I lowered my head. "Let the games begin."

———————

As far as these dinners went, so far, this one wasn't half bad. I was certain it had a lot to do with the woman beside me. I know it had a great deal to do with the fact that I was able to prove the kiss-proof claim as a sham. Only a slight darkening of her lips remained once I finished with Paige before we left the house.

She had to redo her hair as well. I was quite proud of both things. She reapplied her lipstick, and I was determined to prove my theory again before the end of the night. She was too tempting not to.

We were a little late, finding my family at the table already. A couple of bottles of wine were open, and I poured a glass of white for Paige and ordered myself a tonic with lime. I was driving so not drinking, even though I had to admit it would make the night more bearable.

Everyone at the table commented on how lovely Paige looked. My father was especially verbose in his praise. She was embarrassed by their words, meeting my eyes as the color rose in her cheeks. I bent close and kissed the warm skin. "Told you, Sweet Pea."

She sipped her wine, making small talk with my mom, who sat next to her. My dad clapped me on the shoulder. "Did you see there's a dance floor? Your mother and I are going to take full advantage of that."

Maddox groaned and rolled his eyes. "You mean you're going to throw Cami around again?"

My mom chuckled. "Only slow dances tonight, Mad Dog." She shook her finger at my dad. "And don't hold me so tight this time. Remember, I do need to breathe in order to survive."

My dad clutched at his heart. "I'm wounded. Sunshine, I thought all you needed was me."

Beside me, Paige laughed and turned to me. "I see where you get it from."

"The charm?"

"The goofiness."

That made everyone laugh.

I stood and held out my hand. "Let's take a walk."

We strolled the tables, perusing the items up for auction. I kept my questions casual but watched Paige for any sign of desire or interest. She passed the expensive earrings without a second glance and didn't even linger by the spa packages. I decided I needed to get creative.

"I need a birthday gift for Ava," I said. "What about that watch?"

She frowned. "Ava would never wear that. It's too ostentatious."

"Oh. What about that certificate for a shopping spree at—" I squinted "—Today's Madame?"

She snorted. "I don't think your sister wants to dress like a whore."

I grimaced, deciding maybe I was going to strike out. Then I saw Paige's eyes widen and a look of interest flash over her face. I followed her gaze, not surprised to see the one thing that had caught her attention was a little girl's bed that looked like it should belong to a princess. Pink, tufted, with lights and gauzy stuff floating around it. I knew as well as Paige did that Lucy would adore it. I quickly read the details, pleased to see it would be made into a double size and the winner could pick the fabric and other elements. I knew she would never ask me for it, nor could she afford it for Lucy. But I could. We kept walking, and I did spot a great fishing rod for Pops that I placed an outrageous bid on. I also bid on a wine tasting package for four I thought Beth and Paige would enjoy. It was all I could find.

As we approached the table, I waited until Paige sat down, then I strolled over to the bar to get another drink. On the way, I stopped by the bed picture and put a bid on it so high no one would even want to try to outbid me. Then I stood at the end of the line and waited to get another tonic.

Finally, glass in hand, I turned around, bumping into a man. Luckily, the little liquid that spilled only hit my hand. He stepped back, looking askance.

"Sorry," I offered. "Busy space."

He brushed an imaginary splash off his jacket with a frown. "You could be more careful when you pivot. Perhaps imbibe less alcohol."

When you pivot? Imbibe less alcohol? Who the hell spoke like that?

128

Unable to resist, I deepened my voice. "My sincere apologies, my good man. Might I buy you a drink to compensate for my lack of grace?"

His eyes narrowed, and I sipped my tonic to hide my smile. He studied me, so I did the same back. He was familiar, but I wasn't sure why. He was tall and lean. He had lines on his forehead, no doubt from a perpetual frown, and although he appeared about my age, something made him look older. His eyes were cold, and his mouth pressed in a thin line. He looked displeased, and I had a feeling that was his normal expression. He had short, sandy-colored hair shot with gray, dull hazel eyes, and he stood ramrod straight. He reminded me of a drill sergeant in a bad movie. I felt as if I should salute, but I thought he might make me drop and give him fifty for my inexcusable behavior. He wore a thin gold band on his left hand, and I wondered who the poor woman was who was married to him. As he studied me, he constantly flicked his fingers on his right hand in a nervous gesture, and it hit me. He had been present when I had gone to quote a job. His flicking had stuck with me. He had been rude and cutting, demanding the owner of the company show up, not a worker. The way he spat the word was as if it—*as if I*—were beneath him, and it got my back up. I had shut my book and nodded, not bothering to correct him. I didn't want his business.

"I'll be sure to have him contact you."

The quote I sent was astronomical, and I never heard from him again. His name appeared in my head, and I spoke it out loud.

"Alan Forsyth."

He frowned. "Do I know you?"

I wanted to laugh, but I didn't. "We met once."

"I don't recall."

I smirked. "I'm not surprised."

Then he snapped his fingers. "The gardener."

I smirked again. "Right in one."

Before he could say anything else, a horror-filled gasp sounded at my elbow. Startled, I met Paige's wide, panicked eyes. I gripped her arm. "Paige, Sweet Pea, what is it?"

She didn't look at me. Her focus was on the stern-faced jerk in front of me.

"Alan?" she whispered. "What are you doing here?"

A sneer crossed his face as he regarded her. Instinctively, I slid my arm around her waist, drawing her close, her words echoing in my head.

Holy shit.

Standing in front of me, every inch the asshole I thought him to be, was her ex.

"Hello, Paige." He looked between us. "A *gardener?* How very...*you.*"

Then he turned and marched away.

CHAPTER TWELVE
PAIGE

My head spun and the room tilted. If it weren't for Liam's arm holding me up, I was certain my legs would give out. I shook from head to toe in shock.

Liam drew me closer, his voice a low hum in my ear as he pressed a glass to my lips. "Sip this, Paige."

The cold tang of the tonic hit my throat, jolting me. I took another sip and pulled back, meeting Liam's concerned gaze.

"I think I might get sick," I confessed.

"Okay, walk with me slowly."

He guided me out of the suddenly overheated room. We went down the hall and bypassed the main corridor.

"Where—"

He cut me off. "I know a private place."

A moment later, he opened the door and tugged me inside a family bathroom. There was a chair in the corner, and he led me to it, pushing me down. He wet some paper towels in the sink and placed them on my neck. The cool felt good, and his closeness helped diminish the shock I was feeling. He crouched beside me. "Are you going to throw up?"

"No, it's passing."

He pressed his glass into my hand. "Drink more of this."

I sipped the icy cold tonic and leaned my head back. Liam stroked my head gently, his fingers light and comforting on my skin.

"Baby, I'm sorry."

I opened my eyes. "It's not your fault."

"We can leave. You stay here, and I'll go explain to my parents."

I sat up, clutching his hand. "No. You don't have to do that."

"I don't want you in the same room as him. I thought you were going to pass out, you were so pale."

"I don't have to talk to him. There are so many people, I probably won't even see him. He won't seek me out either. We have nothing to say to each other."

I met his eyes. They were filled with nothing but love, worry, and warmth. They were totally different from the cold, flat gaze Alan had.

"Why did he call you a gardener?"

Liam told me about the one time they had met. He paused. "Forsyth? Your last name is Winters."

"He insisted I have my name changed back. He didn't want Lucy attached to him by anything. He paid for it, and I was happy to disassociate myself from him in every fashion."

Liam lowered his head with a shake. He muttered under his breath, then lifted his head, his expression furious. "What a horrible excuse for a human."

"Why were you talking to him?"

His story about Alan's over-the-top reaction and stiff language made me smile. The fact that Liam was actually making fun of him would have gone over Alan's head completely. I huffed out a long sigh.

"Nothing has changed, it seemed, except perhaps he's gotten worse."

"I saw a ring on his hand. I think he's remarried," Liam told me. "I feel sorry for whoever made that mistake."

Gathering my courage, I stood and brushed out my dress. "I do as well. But it doesn't affect me, and I refuse to let him spoil our night. Let's rejoin your family and forget him."

He ran his fingers down my cheek. "Are you sure, Sweet Pea?"

I nodded firmly. "Yes."

He touched his lips to my mouth. "My brave girl. I love you."

I smiled at him, tamping down my nerves. "That is why I *can* do this. I have you."

That earned me another kiss. "Yes, you do."

Hand in hand, we returned to the ballroom.

We ran into Aiden in the hallway. He looked between us, frowning.

"I thought you dragged Paige off to ravish her in some dark corner, but your mother said something was wrong. As usual, she was correct." He put his hand on Liam's shoulder. "What is it?"

"Paige's ex is here. It shocked her, and I took her out of there to help her calm down a little."

Aiden's eyebrows rose. "That scumbag who deserted you is here?" he asked me.

"Yes."

Liam explained his encounter and how he had met Alan before.

"What a pompous ass." Aiden rolled his shoulders and cracked his knuckles. "There's an empty parking lot behind the building. We can lure him there."

Before I could protest, he continued. "I know the kitchen staff pretty well. I could make sure you could spit on his food. Or get some ex-lax shaved onto his dessert. Hmm?"

I couldn't stop my smile. Leaning up, I kissed his cheek. "Thanks, Aiden, but no. I just want to ignore him."

Liam chuckled. "Good ideas, though, Dad. Who is giving the speech tonight?"

"I am."

"It's a pretty special night, right? I'm here with my girl. My business is doing well. BAM is huge... ABC is totally rocking it..." He trailed off.

Aiden grinned. "Such a special night." He clapped Liam on the shoulder. "Words are so much better at times."

I glanced between them, not understanding.

"I'll head back to the table. Your mother will be worried by now." Aiden touched my shoulder. "You come when you're ready."

"Thank you."

He brushed a kiss to my forehead. "We got you, Paige."

I watched him weave his way through the crowded hall and enter the ballroom.

"Your family is so amazing," I murmured.

Liam squeezed my hand. "They consider you family now too, you know. My dad meant what he said. We've got you, and you don't have to face this alone. Alan won't get a chance to upset you again tonight. Ignore him. Don't let him win."

"He thinks I don't belong here."

"He's wrong. You're with me, with my family. You belong by my side, and I won't let him near you. I promise."

I smiled at him, fighting back the emotional tears that threatened. "I know."

"Remember that. You're with us and you're safe. You belong. You ready to do this?"

"Yes."

We headed into the room, the noise level rising tenfold. I kept my head up, refusing to cower. Alan had no control over me anymore. I wasn't going to allow him to ruin the night. I had Liam beside me, and I knew without a doubt he wouldn't leave my side again tonight. I was safe.

At the table, I slid into my seat beside Cami. It was obvious Aiden had already filled everyone in, and they regarded me with kind smiles. Cami slipped her arm around my shoulders and hugged me. "Are you all right?"

"I'm fine."

Aiden leaned over. "Asshole eleven o'clock. Don't be obvious when you look—he's been staring since you walked in."

Beside me, Liam draped his napkin over his lap and leaned his arm on the back of my chair. He muttered under his breath, and I knew he'd spotted Alan. My hand trembled a little as I picked up my wine and took a sip, daring to glance up. Four tables across from ours, directly in my line of vision, I was met with Alan's flat, frosty glare. Sitting beside him was, I assumed, his wife. She sat, her spine straight, her shoulders perfectly squared, and had a bored, discontented look on her face. She wasn't paying any attention to Alan, and he seemed to be ignoring her. They sat apart from each other, as if being close were unthinkable. As if he knew what I was thinking, Liam's hand tightened on my shoulder, and he drew me closer, dropping a kiss to my head. I tilted my head toward him with a smile, and he lowered his head and dropped a fast kiss to my mouth. As I glanced back, I saw Alan's gaze had narrowed, focusing intently on our table, and unable to help myself, I lifted my glass in a silent toast and smirked at him.

Instantly, he dropped his gaze and half turned in his seat. Beside me, Cami chuckled.

"Good move, sweetheart. Don't let him make you uncomfortable. He can go fuck himself."

I widened my eyes at her words, but she shrugged. "Katy's favorite saying. It comes in handy."

Aiden burst out laughing and kissed her. "That's my woman. Blunt and direct."

Bentley rose and left the table, and I made a concerted effort to join in on the conversation. There was lots of talk about family, upcoming plans for the summer, and a pending visit from Richard VanRyan and his wife, Katy. I had heard a lot about them, especially from their daughter Grace, and I was looking forward to meeting them. It was obvious that he and Maddox were especially close, and I had a feeling lots of shenanigans ensued when they were all together. Many people stopped by the table, shaking hands with the BAM members, talking for a moment or two, then drifting away. On occasion, I stole a glance Alan's direction, trying not to laugh at his not-so-subtle way of spying on our group. I knew he was curious who was at the table and why it was such an attraction. No one stopped by his table or spoke to him or his wife—even the other people seated with him. They seemed to make no attempt to interact either, and I wondered if Alan thought the people around him were beneath him. He often did.

Bentley returned, sliding into his seat as they announced dinner would be served in ten minutes. He picked up his drink. "Mr. and Mrs. Forsyth are here as guests of the Image Corporation. He's a management analyst?" He looked at me to confirm, and I nodded. "Mrs. Forsyth is the daughter of Wayne Wallis, the CEO of the company Alan works for." He paused, taking a sip of his wine. "Apparently they are both a handful." He met my gaze. "And neither of them is important to our evening or this event. So, let's forget they even exist, shall we? I, for one, am all about having a great time with my family this evening."

My heart warmed at his words and the hidden meaning behind them. Bentley raised his glass, and everyone at the table copied him. We toasted to a great evening, and I turned in my seat, studiously ignoring the man across the room. It took everything in me to pretend he hadn't upset me, but I was determined not to let him see that. Not to let him win again. He no longer mattered. The wonderful man sitting next to me did.

LIAM

I controlled my anger as best I could, pushing it down and copying my family's behavior. My dad was extra outrageous, making everyone laugh, and the mirth was loud. I couldn't help but watch Alan on occasion. He and his wife sent their dinner back three times and, even when the plate was deemed acceptable, barely picked at it. I noticed they never touched and rarely spoke, and I could only imagine the silence and cold they lived with on a daily basis. A huge part of me was grateful for Alan's callous nature since it meant it wasn't Paige beside him, silent and miserable. I had a feeling he was a brutal management analyst, cutting jobs and costs with no regard for the human element. I couldn't imagine him around Lucy. I shuddered simply thinking about it.

Since our amusement seemed to annoy Alan, I made sure to encourage my dad and his antics. I knew Paige was still struggling, despite her efforts to seem otherwise. Her shoulders were tense, and her fingers held her wineglass too tightly. She ate her dinner, but her actions were reflex. She chewed and swallowed, but I doubted she tasted a thing.

I seethed inside, wishing I could simply walk up to him and drag him outside to teach him a lesson. But I also knew that wasn't possible. All I could do was be there for Paige and make sure to drive home the message she was far better off without him.

My dad helped get that message across—very effectively.

Between dinner and dessert, there were always a couple of speeches. Because BAM was such a major contributor, they were usually asked to be one of the speakers. I listened as the emcee spoke of BAM, their tireless work against bullying, the outreach programs they sponsored, their generous donations of time and money to many causes, and the excellence of their business. Then he invited Dad up to the podium to speak. As he went past me, Dad squeezed my shoulder. He stepped up to the microphone, smiling widely at the crowd. He began with his usual spiel, thanking the organizers, all the catering staff, everyone involved with the event. He leaned on the podium, looking relaxed and at ease.

"I'm going to get a little personal for a moment, so indulge me. Tonight's event is close to our hearts at BAM because, at the core, it's about family. We're all about that. I have been blessed in my life to have people in it who became family. I have my own family too. A wonderful wife who makes me smile every day because of how special she is. Friends I call brothers. I get to work with my kids." He waved his hand toward our table. "My son, Liam Callaghan, runs his own company—Branching Outward. Trust me, folks, you want the best landscaping company in the province? He's your man. I've lost count of the number of awards he's received, and I'm damn proud of him." He paused. "Here's a shameless plug while I'm at it. It's not too late to put in a bid on his donation. Last time I looked, the page was getting full, so I suggest you don't let the opportunity pass you by. Only an idiot would let that happen." His tone was teasing, but his stare was focused on Alan before he finished. "It's a great cause, and you'll be the envy of your entire neighborhood."

I tried not to laugh at his not-too-subtle dig. Alan now knew, without a doubt, who I was. He'd dismissed me as a gardener twice. He wouldn't be happy knowing he was wrong.

Dad kept going. "I'm sitting with my family, and we're all honored to be part of this evening. To make it even more special, my son brought his girl. We consider her the newest member of our family, and we're all thrilled she agreed to join us tonight. She is bright, beautiful, and to top it off, her little Lucy has totally captured our hearts. So, Paige, thanks for putting up with my son, and welcome to the BAM clan. I hope to have you with us at many more of these fabulous events."

Paige startled at his words, but my smile was huge. As with Evan, my family had just claimed her outright. She was part of us. Under our protection. Unable to help myself, I pulled her close and kissed her. She gazed up at me in wonder.

"Your family," she breathed.

"Loves you," I finished for her.

I spared a glance at Alan. He was furious. What I thought was a frown before was now a deep scowl indicating his unhappiness. His glare was directed at Paige, and I held her close so there was no mistake. He'd get nowhere near her. Ever. And he knew her life was far better than his—and there was nothing he could do about it.

Dad finished off with more encouragement to donate, pushed the auction, and praised the charity. His speech was clear, short, and perfect. He returned to the table amid a round of applause, and I had to blink again when Paige stood and flung her arms around his neck. He grinned, lifting her off her feet as he hugged her back. Mom laughed as she watched them, and even Bentley chuckled. After Dad sat down, Bent lifted his glass.

"Good job, Aiden. Hardly any cursing."

Dad lifted his glass. "I had an important message to send. I think it was received."

I toasted him with a smile. "Loud and clear."

CHAPTER THIRTEEN
LIAM

The dinner finished and the music began. I was surprised when Paige didn't ask to leave. Instead, I led her to the floor and held her in my arms, swaying to the soft music. She had relaxed once Alan stood after dessert and disappeared. His wife left not long after, and I assumed they had departed. Good riddance.

After I danced with her, Dad, Maddox, and Bentley all took her for a spin. I laughed watching her with Dad—he was extra careful, moving in small circles, unlike the wild way he liked to move. I danced with Mom and my aunts, enjoying a few moments with each of them. They all thought Paige was wonderful, and I had to agree. A text told me I was the winner of all the items I had bid on, and I told my mom about my plans with the bed. Her eyes lit up. "She'll love it!"

"I know."

"How long does it take?"

"The form said a couple of weeks."

"We can paint the room. Liv is better with colors than I am."

"I'll call her."

I danced with Paige again, noticing she was looking tired. "You almost ready to go home?" I asked.

"I don't want to cut your evening short," she replied.

"I would far rather go home, get comfortable, and eat pizza with you and my family than stay here. Trust me. Dad will agree. He goes to hundreds of these things, and they get boring fast."

"I'd like that."

I traced a finger down her cheek. "You were beautiful for me tonight, Sweet Pea. Thank you."

Her hands tightened on me. "Thank you for what you did."

"No thanks are needed."

I led her to the table. "We're going to head out."

Dad grinned. "We were just discussing that. I'm going to stop at Dom's for pizza. We'll be at the Hub if you want to join us."

"Great. I have to go grab my auction items."

"I'm going to slip to the ladies' room," Paige murmured. "I'll meet you at the car?"

"I'll wait by the door."

She rolled her eyes. "You're not insisting on coming in with me? He's obviously gone, just like any bad smell does. I'll meet you at the car."

I shrugged. I'd wait by the door anyway.

It took me a few minutes to get the certificates for the wine tasting and pick up the fishing rod. I got the information I needed to contact the maker of the bed and hurried to the door. Paige wasn't there, but I noticed lots of women heading down the hall and assumed the ladies' room was a busy place. I waited longer, then decided to go stick the fishing rod in the trunk and come back.

Except as I went around the corner of the building, I spotted a man arguing with a woman. The overhead light reflected on her dress, the vivid blue telling me exactly who she was. Rage overtook me as I realized Alan was holding Paige's arm and shaking her while he cursed and yelled. Without a thought, I broke into a run, skidding to halt as I watched Paige suddenly step back and land a punch to his face, then plant a perfectly aimed knee into his crotch. He went over like a sack of potatoes, landing on the asphalt with a loud groan. I covered the last few feet, reaching for Paige.

"Are you all right?"

She shook her head, smoothing her hair. "I am now." She glared at Alan's sprawled figure. "I'll be better once I speak my mind."

Alan grunted from the pavement, struggling to get to his feet. Blood spurted from his nose, and he clutched his balls in agony. I lifted my foot, pressing down on his shoulder. "I'd stay down where you belong, you little maggot. I think the lady has something to say, and I have a feeling she has no problem taking another swing at you." I hunched over him. "And this time, I'd help."

I kept my foot on his shoulder as I straightened up. "Sweet Pea, the floor is yours."

She crossed her arms. Her voice was direct and clear. "All these years, I've hated you. For how you treated me, what you said about my daughter—the total disregard you had for her, for her life. But after tonight, I realized I don't hate you at all."

I was surprised by her words.

"You mean *nothing*. I can't hate *nothing*. You are worthless. You're a nasty, lonely, sad little man trying to prove to the world you're something else." She crouched down. "*My* daughter? She is the most amazing little person. And the best part is she has nothing of you in her. *Not a thing*. She is sunshine and light. Filled with love and goodness. She is *all* me."

I clapped slowly. "I'll second that."

Alan glared at her, not speaking. He pressed his fingers to the bridge of his nose, trying to stanch the blood. He still grimaced every time he shifted, and I felt a flash of pride at how hard she must have kicked him.

"She is going to go forward in this world and make it better. She is going to do great things. Without any help from you. You know, she's never even asked me about you. Her little life is so full, she has no need." She looked at me and smiled. "Especially since this wonderful man came into our world. He is everything you aren't. Warm, loving, generous. He doesn't see what's wrong with her or me. He only sees what's right. We both love him so much."

Our eyes locked, and my heart rate picked up. Every time I didn't think I could fall more in love with this woman, she proved me wrong.

"So, thanks, Alan, for being such an ass. Because of you, I found a real man to love. Lucy found someone who accepts her for just being Lucy—which is pretty damn perfect. We're both so happy."

She laughed. "Once again, the exact opposite of you. But that's how it's always been. I'm glad to be out of it."

She held out her hand. "Can we go home now, Liam?"

I couldn't help the little kick my foot made as I lifted it off Alan's shoulder. I took her hand, and we began to walk away as he struggled to sit. "Bitch," he sneered, the sound muffled, but I heard it.

I turned and walked back. He hadn't realized I could hear him. He shook his head, panic flaring in his eyes. I crouched down close, smelling his fear. "Remember something. *Landscaping.* I own the company. I think you figured that out from my dad, right? It requires a lot of dirt and big machines. I have it all. You so much as breathe her name, appear accidentally any place she is at? I *ever* see you around her or Lucy? I will find you and bury you so deep, you will never be discovered." I met his terrified eyes. "They are mine. I protect what is mine. That's what *gardeners* do. *We bury shit.*" I stood. "Are we clear?"

I smelled the urine before I saw the puddle under him. As I expected, a bully was never as brave when his opponent was bigger than him.

I took Paige's hand. "I think we're done."

She didn't look back. "I think so too."

I got her in the car and out of the parking lot fast. In my rearview mirror, I saw Alan hobbling across the lot toward his car. I had no idea where his wife was and, frankly, didn't care. I was done thinking about him.

I saw Paige flex her hand with a grimace.

"Sore, tiger?"

She giggle-hiccupped, followed by a sob, and I pulled into the parking lot of a convenience store. I hurried in, grabbed a bag of frozen peas, and tossed some money on the counter, not worrying about the change. I opened her door and crouched beside her, examining her hand. The knuckles were a little swollen, and I could see she was going to bruise. I wrapped the peas around her hand and wiped the tears from her cheeks.

"Are you okay, Sweet Pea?"

She nodded. "I-I'm fine. A little shaky."

"The adrenaline rush is fading. Your right hook is pretty impressive. And we might need to register your foot as a lethal weapon. Alan's gonna have some pretty sore junk for the next while."

She laughed, the sound slightly frantic, and I decided I needed to get her home. Now.

Back in the car, I held her hand.

"Do you want to tell me what prompted that?"

She leaned her head back with a sigh. "I came out of the ladies' room and you weren't there, so I thought you'd headed to the car to put the things in the trunk. I thought I'd save you a trip back in."

"The line was a little longer than I expected."

"I figured that, but before I could come back, Alan suddenly appeared."

"What happened?"

"He was his usual caustic self. Called me a few names, informed me hanging with rich people didn't make me any better than him. He let me know that once you were tired of me, I'd be cast to the side. That I would never really fit in."

I tightened my hands on the wheel but remained silent.

"I told him that, even without you, I was better than him since I was a decent person." She swallowed and looked out the window. "I tried to walk away, but he grabbed me. I think he'd been drinking, which Alan never used to do since it meant he might lose control. I smelled alcohol on his breath, though, and his eyes were unfocused." She paused. "I told him to let go, but he refused. His grip was really tight, and he tore one of the sleeves of your mom's dress. That really pissed me off."

"My mom can fix the dress," I assured her.

"He acted as if he had the right to touch me. To push me around and say anything he wanted because I was beneath him. I always had been in his eyes—or at least, to the man he became after we were married. That made me angrier, and then…"

"Then what?"

"He called Lucy 'that thing with the grotesque deformity.' He assured me you would walk away soon enough, once you got tired of slumming and feeling pity for us." She sucked in a deep breath. "I couldn't stand hearing him call my daughter names. Disparaging you." Her voice rose. "She isn't grotesque! She's-she's—" Her sob cut off her voice.

I squeezed her hand. "She's perfect just the way she is, Paige."

"Yes. And you are so wonderful. I've never felt so much rage. I was livid. Suddenly I remembered everything from a self-defense course I took years ago. The maneuvers Ava showed me. I moved without thinking, and suddenly, he was on the ground and you were there." Another sob escaped her throat. "I lied when I said I didn't hate him. I loathe that man." She lowered her head as the tears came, sobbing into her hands.

I pulled into the compound and headed to the house. I flung open my door and went to hers, lifting her out of the car and heading inside. I sat her on the bathroom counter and wrapped her in my arms, letting her get the emotion out. "My fierce little warrior," I crooned. "Defending the people you love. Lucy and I are lucky to have you in our corners."

"I've never hit anyone before."

"You did well, baby. You knocked him for a loop. His nose is never gonna look the same." I chuckled. "Never mind his balls."

She half giggled, half sobbed, and I lifted her head, cradling her face. "No more tears. He isn't worth it, and he deserved it."

"What-what if he presses charges or something?"

I fingered the torn sleeve of the dress and focused on the bruises forming on the arm he'd gripped. "If he does, we'll have this documented. It was self-defense. But I doubt he will—his overinflated ego won't allow him to tell the world he got taken down by a little slip of a woman."

I wrapped her in my arms again, letting her lean on me. When she was fully relaxed, I pressed a kiss to her head. "Tell me what you want. Bath and bed? Ice cream and a movie?"

"I thought we were having pizza?"

"I wasn't sure you were up to more of my family."

"No, I want to. I don't want Alan to ruin any more of tonight than he has."

"Okay. Let's change and head over. I want my dad to look at your hand."

She sniffled, wiping her cheeks. "Okay."

CHAPTER FOURTEEN
PAIGE

Aiden checked my hand, moving the fingers carefully.

"Nothing broken," he assured me, wrapping a fresh bag of ice around it. "One hell of a punch, though, slugger. I'm proud of you."

"For hitting a human being?" I asked.

He leaned on the chair, meeting my eyes. His mismatched gaze was serious. As serious as I had ever seen Aiden be. "No," he said. "For slaying your Goliath. He deserved that punch and kick to his balls. You said your piece. Now you can move on. Chapter closed."

"I hope he doesn't make trouble for you or Liam."

He scoffed and straightened up, tugging me out of the chair. "His nose will heal fine, and eventually, his balls will crawl out of his stomach. But he won't forget your strength. That will leave a lasting impression. And I agree with Liam—he will never admit a little slip of a girl did this. He'll say he was mugged or some other nonsense." He hugged me close. "Don't give it a second thought."

I sat down beside Cami. She patted my hand. "Don't worry about the dress. I can fix it easily, and you can wear it again."

"I thought it was a loan."

She smiled. "No, I fitted it for you. It's yours."

"Thank you."

She leaned forward, lowering her voice. "Aiden is right. Shake tonight off. Don't let Alan interfere with the new life you have found with Liam. Think of it as a cleansing. You finally got to use your voice and let him know he failed. You're stronger, better, and more resilient than he believed. He thought he'd broken you, and now he knows he was wrong. That alone will drive him crazy." She winked. "If you want to make sure of it, marry Liam, give me more Lucys. Be so happy, you forget everything but now."

"Um, we haven't talked marriage."

She laughed. "You will. I know my son."

Liam walked over, carrying a slice of pizza. "What are you two whispering about?"

Cami smiled. "We're talking about you, dear. That's all you need to know."

He grinned. "Well, I am spectacular."

Cami snorted. "In your own mind, yes. Now bring your mother a slice of pizza. The chicken was extra rubbery this evening. Even your father had trouble choking it down."

"I noticed he only ate two helpings," Liam said dryly.

"I had to keep up my strength," Aiden insisted, joining in. "Your mother wanted to dance."

I met Liam's eyes, both of us trying not to laugh. It wasn't Cami who wanted to dance. Aiden loved to "cut a rug," as he called it, and dragged her to the dance floor every chance he got. She simply held on for dear life. Luckily, Liam and her other children inherited her grace and not Aiden's.

"Pizza, Sweet Pea?" Liam asked, his voice quiet. I knew he was looking at my arm, his anger still simmering. He hated to see the bruises. He was furious Alan had even touched me, never mind left marks. My hand wrapped in ice was a further reminder of the end of the evening.

I made a decision. Cami was right. I wasn't going to let Alan spoil this for us. He was done.

"Please. Two pieces. I'm starving. And a beer would be welcome."

His smile was wide. "Yeah?"

I leaned back in the chair. "Yeah."

He bent over and kissed me. "You got it."

Lucy was full of news when we went to Ava's to pick her up the next morning.

"We ate wings, Momma! We watched Nemo and had popcorn," she told me, clutching my neck and talking fast as if she might forget a detail. "And look at my toes!"

I grinned at the sparkling nails.

"I did Ava's for her," she said. "She said I did the best job evah."

I glanced at Ava's feet, trying not to laugh. The polish looked as if it had been applied by a drunken person. In the dark. But Ava grinned. "Evah," she agreed. Then she chuckled. "You should see Gracie's."

I grinned, and Lucy stretched toward Liam, entirely content to rest in his arms. She repeated the conversation, adding details she had missed in her excitement. Her bubble bath in the big tub. The soda Ava let her have with dinner. The cinnamon toast Ava made her this morning at six.

"We had a morning nap," she told Liam. "Ava says it's a rule here. You hafta have a nap on Sunday mornings." She cupped his ear, not lowering her voice, but thinking their conversation private now. "I not really sleep, I just pretend. Ava did."

"Did she snore?" Liam whispered back, cupping her ear, his hand encompassing her whole head.

"Yes." Lucy made a little snorting sound. "Like that. It made Mr. Teddy laugh."

Ava chuckled. "Pretty accurate. I've heard myself do that."

"You coming for brunch?" Liam inquired.

Ava yawned. "Later."

"Another nap?" I asked quietly, knowing Sundays were the day she liked to sleep in.

"Yeah. If there's any Danish left, snag me one and hide it from Dad. He's like a hoover around those."

"I will." I hugged her. "Thank you."

Her hazel eyes, unique and beautiful as she was, were soft. "Anytime. Really. I had a blast with her. She is such an awesome kid." Then she tapped my hand. "And so is her mom."

I knew Liam had told Ava what happened. I smiled and shrugged. "Thanks for your tips."

She winked. "Anytime."

Monday, Liam showed up with lunch. I was on a call, and he waited patiently until I finished. He insisted on looking at my hand even though I told him it was fine. He'd hovered all day yesterday, even driving his parents crazy. Aiden dragged him off to run on the beach so I could relax with Lucy and Cami. Ronan and Beth dropped by, and we all ended up in the pool. It was a fun, relaxed day, even with the hovering.

I finally convinced him my hand was fine by wrapping my fingers around his cock and stroking it. That led to another type of hovering, and when he left, we were both smiling and more at ease.

And the week continued. He would appear at some point, lunch in hand. I would hear his truck and wait with anticipation. Sometimes we'd eat and talk. Other times, he'd pull me toward my room, the glint in his eyes unmistakable. He was passionate and demanding, his lovemaking thorough and complete. One day, he insisted we sit outside and enjoy the day, and we both took the afternoon off. On Thursday, I texted him in the morning, telling him not to bring lunch. Instead, I made him macaroni and cheese, having heard him tell Beth that was one of his favorites. He devoured the dish, the smile never leaving his face.

After he finished, he sat across from me, playing with my fingers.

"I have something to ask," he said.

"Sure."

"I was wondering if I could have you and Lucy this weekend. Pick you up tomorrow and keep you with me in Port Albany."

"Wow. We would love that. Lucy will be beside herself."

"There's a bed in the guest room. Not much else."

"I'm sure she can bring a few friends to keep her company," I said dryly. "She has a couple to pick from."

"Okay, I'll pick you up around four. It probably means I won't be around for lunch."

"You don't have to come for lunch every day, Liam. I know you work all over the city and the outskirts. I don't expect you to keep rearranging your schedule."

He smiled, still playing with my fingers. "I like it. Lunch is ours. I share you with Lucy and everyone else in the evenings. I like knowing I get to have just you for a bit every day."

"You must hate all the driving."

He met my eyes. "No. The only thing I hate is saying goodbye and leaving you. I dislike it at lunch, I hate it at night. I look forward to the day I don't have to."

Every time he showed his love, every time he said something unexpectedly sweet about our future, my doubts faded. Little pieces of them disappeared as if they had never existed. I wanted to tell him that, but the words didn't come. All I could do was smile.

"One day."

He nodded and stood. "I have to go. I have consultations tonight, so I won't see you until tomorrow." He kissed me, long and hard. "I'll call you later, though, and I'll see you tomorrow at four. You, me, and the munchkin all weekend."

He paused before he went out the door. "And, Paige?"

I looked up. "Yeah?"

"That one day? It's gonna be soon."

Then he was gone.

I stared at the door for a long time.

Lucy's laughter filled the pool area, her high-pitched squeal of glee piercing the air as Aiden and Liam tossed her back and forth like a football. A special football. They were only a few feet apart in the pool and she barely left one set of arms before the next caught her, but she was loving every moment. Aiden caught her, settling her on his shoulder.

"All right, Lucy-loo. Time to swim."

He had been teaching her, never rushed or impatient. She could paddle a little, but he showed her how to kick her feet and move through the water. A pool noodle under her arms helped keep her afloat. He told me earlier he was investigating different techniques to help one-armed swimmers. He was quiet for a few moments, then lowered his voice.

"You ever considered a bionic-type arm? For when she is a little older?" he asked.

"Maybe one day. She hates wearing the prosthesis she has. The War Amps were great with their programs and help and we tried a few, but she has always done better on her own. She has to want it."

"She might surprise you one day." He studied her. "They've made great progress with them."

"If it helps her, I'm all for it."

He nodded. "Good to know."

He joined Liam and Lucy in the pool via a cannonball and joined back in their fun. Watching them together, they looked like a family. Lucy seemed to resemble Liam more all the time, her smiles as wide as his, her hazel eyes filled with laughter. She had started copying his gestures, even taken to using a few of his sayings.

"It's what family does, Momma," she informed me seriously when I thanked her for taking her plate to the sink.

"Need to feed the seed!" She would announce after supper daily. Liam had helped her plant a tiny garden out front, and she religiously watered her little plants every day, getting quite upset when it would rain and steal her tiny moments of pleasure.

The day she murmured "Holy shit" was the day I made Liam sit down and explain what bad words those were and how ashamed he was of having used them. She made Evan tell her all the bad words, and now a swear jar sat on the kitchen counter. Liam and Ronan filled it often. She became a keen listener to their quiet conversations and loved the sound the coins made when they went into the jar. I had a feeling it would pay for her first year of university.

Later, we sat on the beach by the fire, toasting marshmallows after having eaten our weight in hot dogs. I sat against Liam's chest, relaxed and warm, watching the fire dance under the stars. The sound of the water lapping at the shore was rhythmic and soothing. Ronan brought Beth and Evan out once she was done at work, and they sat across from us, talking quietly. Evan and Lucy made s'mores, laughing and giggling about some secret.

It was bliss.

Liam's lips were warm on my ear. "Happy, Sweet Pea?"

"Yes."

"We'll do this a lot, you know. Lazy weekends, fires, marshmallows, all of it. This is just the start of our life. Our future."

"Hmm," I said, sleepy and content. I knew what he was doing. Tempting me with the future he wanted for us.

"And after the munchkin goes to bed, I'll show you something else we'll be doing a lot of."

I wiggled my ass, feeling his cock respond.

He bit down on my lobe. "Careful, baby. You're playing with fire."

I looked up. "Maybe I want to get burned."

His mouth covered mine. "Now you've done it."

Sunday was considered an unofficial family day at the compound. That was the day most of the kids seemed to show up to visit their parents, Nan and Pops, and one another. Liam explained you never knew who would be there, or when they would show up. Nothing was planned. In the summer, people hung out by the pool in the sun, or at the Hub on rainy days or when the sun became sweltering. It amazed me that a family who mostly worked together and saw one another a lot still chose to hang out on their days off, but as I discovered, this was a special group. They genuinely liked one another.

We'd had coffee on the deck, the sun shining and bright. Liam and Ronan had devoured the pastries on the table, making me laugh. "Are you ever full there, Tree Trunk?"

Emmy leaned forward and looked at me with wide eyes. "What did you call Liam?"

I laughed. "He's like a tree. Strong and tall."

"I always called Aiden Tree Trunk. Although my reasons were a little different." She sat back with a grin. "Like father, like son. We've come full circle."

Everyone laughed. I guessed we had.

I watched Aiden, Maddox, and Van man the grills, the scent of burgers, chicken, and sausages filling the air. It was an impromptu lunch for everyone who had shown up. Beth and I helped gather some condiments for the meal, while Dee and Emmy put together a salad.

"You must keep supplies on hand," I mused.

Emmy laughed. "Sunday is unofficial, but it's rare that it doesn't happen. We always have supplies in the freezers for the barbecue, and the fridge is always full of easy stuff for salads or snacks. Someone here is always hungry."

Cami grinned. "And if you run out of something in your own house, this place is well stocked—saves trips to the grocery store when you realize you're out of carrots!"

I loved these women and their closeness. The way they accepted me as one of them. How they welcomed Lucy. For the first time in my life, I felt part of something. A family. It was a new feeling

—one that would take some getting used to, but I liked it. I simply had to figure out my place.

"Look at that," Cami whispered, staring out the window.

I peeked over her shoulder, smiling at the sight.

Liam was standing talking to Ronan, their heads close as they schemed something. Lucy was cradled in Liam's arms, her head right in there with them. Her arm was wrapped around his neck, looking tiny and pale on his tanned skin. Ronan had his arm around Evan's shoulder, and the boy was looking at Ronan as if he hung the moon.

"They're building their families," Cami murmured. "Look how happy they are."

Beth and I shared a glance. Cami sniffled a little and smiled at us. "I'm so grateful they found you girls. What joy you have brought to all of us."

My place was suddenly clear—and another little doubt broke away.

CHAPTER FIFTEEN
PAIGE

It was hard to go back to the little house in Toronto. It felt cramped and lonely compared to the open spaces of Port Albany. Liam had kissed me long and lingeringly before he left. He had an early morning meeting in Port Albany and wasn't staying the night. I felt restless without him, and after tucking Lucy in, came outside to sit on the step. Beth joined me not long after.

She handed me a glass of wine, and we sat quietly.

"I never noticed the noise here until now," she murmured. "The traffic, the people."

"I know." I glanced up. "You can't see the stars the same way either."

"I wonder what the neighbors would do if we started a fire on the lawn."

I chuckled. "Not the same without the sand and the water."

She nudged me. "Not the same without Ronan and Liam, you mean."

I pulled my knees up to my chest and rested my chin on them. I turned my face her way and grinned. "Definitely not."

"Those Callaghan boys certainly take over your thoughts."

"They take over everything."

She grinned and lifted her glass. "And aren't we glad they do?"

I clinked my glass to hers. "Yes, yes, we are."

———

Monday, Liam appeared, carrying a bag of sandwiches. Beth and I had given him and Ronan each a key, so when I heard the front door open, I signed off, hoping it was Liam. He strode in, his gaze intent. The lunch was tossed on the table as he came toward me, the hunger in his eyes for more than food obvious. Before I could even speak, he swooped me into his arms, his mouth hard on mine. He carried me to the bedroom, placing me on my bed, his body following me down to the mattress. His desire was evident in the tension of his body, his demanding, drugging kiss, and the hardness of his erection pressed between us. I returned his passion with my own, an undeniable hunger for him exploding as soon as he walked in. It felt as if it had been months, not a mere day, since he'd touched me. Since our skin had slid together as he took me. Everything felt magnified as we fumbled and pulled at the clothing separating us. He wasted no time settling between my legs, thrusting inside me. I was so ready for him I ached with it. I threw back my head at the feeling of him. Hot steel encased in velvet. Gliding, stroking, filling me up. Our moans filled the room, his grunts and growls of satisfaction low and sexy. I came quickly, the sensations too much to bear, and he followed not long after, my name falling from his lips as he stiffened and shook. He collapsed on me, our skin damp from exertion, our bodies temporarily sated. He rose on his elbows, gazing down at me. He claimed my mouth in a long, sweet kiss.

"Hi, Sweet Pea. How's your Monday?"

I wrapped my arms around his neck, playing with the thick strands of his hair. "It got better."

He chuckled. "I missed you."

"Really? You hid it so well."

"My bed is far too big without you in it. I barely slept last night."

"Well, this one is never too big when you're around."

He laughed and sat up, looking at the clothing tossed around the room as if caught in a windstorm.

"Wow. I came at you, didn't I?"

"Hmm, you did. I didn't object, though."

He pulled me to his lap, holding me close. "Should I apologize?"

"Nope."

He lifted my chin and kissed me, his tongue stroking mine in long, sensuous passes. "You hungry?" he whispered, ghosting his hands along my sides, cupping my breasts, and rolling my nipples. Turning, I straddled his hips, draping my arms over his massive shoulders. He was obviously hungry again—and not for food.

"Soon," I whispered, kissing my way down his neck. "Soon."

Tuesday was much the same, although he showed some restraint since I was on a call when he arrived. He did pull his chair close, kissing his way up my arm and nuzzling at my neck, silently driving me wild until I was able to sign off and throw myself at him. We never made it to the bedroom that time.

Wednesday, he walked in, sitting beside me when he saw I was on the phone again. Hastily, I scribbled him a note before he got it in his mind to start kissing and caressing me.

Lucy home.

He frowned and mouthed the word *Why?*

Not feeling well, I wrote.

Then I indicated the headset.

Problem customer. Sorry.

I waited for the look of disappointment to cross his face. I figured knowing I couldn't concentrate on him, he'd eat his lunch and leave to go back to work. But instead, I saw only concern. He stood and left the room, and I heard him mutter something about noticing Lucy didn't eat as many tacos as usual the night before. Listening to him, I missed what the customer said and had to ask them to repeat themselves. I shut out everything else and focused on the task at hand. Finally, I was able to hang up, and I headed down the hall, wondering what was going on. Liam hadn't reappeared. I stopped in the doorway of Lucy's room, my heart speeding up at the sight before me. Liam was propped against Lucy's headboard, his body too big for her bed. His feet hung off the end, and he filled the small mattress completely. She was asleep on his chest, her head resting against his shoulder. Mr. Teddy was tucked up with them, and Fluffy the unicorn shared the little space he had on the pillow. Liam stroked her back, rocking slightly as he hummed to her, his eyes shut, oblivious to my presence.

I had barely been able to get her to settle all morning. Her fever made her cranky, and she was restless. But in Liam's arms, she rested, safe and secure.

He opened his eyes, smiling at me.

"She needed a snuggle," he whispered.

"You've been 'snuggling' for over thirty minutes."

He shrugged, careful not to disturb her. "I canceled everything this afternoon. I'll stay with her so you can work."

"You didn't—"

He cut me off. "I wanted to." He pressed a kiss to her hair. "I don't like seeing her sick."

"It's a little bug. She'll be fine. Kids get them."

"I still don't like it."

I bent over, feeling her head. "She's cooler."

"I put a cold cloth on her head, and I got her to drink a little. She passed out after that."

"You're so good to us."

He smiled. "You make that easy. Go eat your sandwich I brought, and I'll be out in a while. I want to make sure she's okay."

I saw the sincerity in his eyes. Holding her, taking care of her wasn't a burden. It never would be for him. He would never find caring for someone he loved a chore.

The last little piece of my doubt broke off and disappeared.

The next while, life had a new pattern. Most days, I saw Liam for lunch. It was, as he said, our time. We talked and laughed, and the more I got to know him, the more I fell. He was genuine. Honest. Completely forthright in his words and deeds. The evenings, the house was usually full. Ronan and Liam were often there. We'd take turns going out while the other couple stayed home with Evan and Lucy. We went out as a group together. Ronan and Liam loved to bowl, go to movies, and do all sorts of things we were never able to afford. Watching them be patient with Evan's leg or Lucy's arm as they showed them how to roll a ball in the bowling alley, or the treats they snuck to them at the movie theater made my heart warm. Weekends became the time we spent in Port Albany.

All too soon, school was out, and day care was done for Lucy. Beth and I had pooled our resources and found some day camps for each of them, but the rest of the time, they would be home. Once again, I assumed Liam would stop showing up for lunch when the kids were home, but as usual, he surprised me. Tuesday became his afternoon with them. He took them out, visiting parks, playgrounds, gardens, and arcades. The local swimming pool. When he could, Ronan joined him. My regard for them grew every passing week. My love for Liam deepened, strengthened, and I couldn't imagine my life without him in it.

We sat on the steps, a rare day when the house was empty except for us. Beth and Ronan were in Port Albany. Both kids were with them—Lucy having one of her girls' nights with Ava. I was pretty sure Cami would join them, maybe even Emmy and Dee. They were all incredibly fond of Lucy, who lapped up the attention. Liam had arranged for Ronan to bring Lucy back tomorrow night, and we were staying in Toronto. Although I would miss the interaction with the family, the thought of Liam to myself until tomorrow evening was too tempting to resist.

I sighed as I settled against his chest. I rested my arms on his strong thighs and enjoyed the unexpectedly cool air that followed the rain of the last couple of days. It was a nice change.

Liam stroked his fingers up and down my arms, his touch leaving a trail of warmth. I gripped his knees, my hands hardly fitting around the large muscles.

He sighed and bent low. "I want to show you something."

I glanced up, seeing the nervous expression on his face.

"Okay."

He took out his phone and scanned through it, holding it in front of us. I studied the picture, the familiarity of it striking me.

"That's like that bed we saw at the auction."

"It is. I bought it and had it made for Lucy. For her room in Port Albany."

"You spoil her, Liam." I took the phone, studying the image. "It's so pretty, she'll never want to leave."

"That was part of my plan."

I froze, my hand midair in the act of returning the phone to him. "Pardon me?"

He shifted so our eyes met. "I want Lucy in that room permanently. I want you there every day." He sucked in a deep breath. "I want you to move in with me."

I stared at him, part of me not surprised to hear the words, yet still shocked.

"Liam—"

He cut me off. "Listen to me before you say no. I love you, Paige. I love Lucy. I think about you all the time when we're not together. When I'm with you, I'm complete. When we're all together, we're a family. I want that all the time. I want to hear Lucy running around the house. Laughing and squealing when she's excited. I want to protect her, watch her grow. Be there when she's sick." He took my hands in his. "I want to be there for you. Every single day."

"But Beth and Evan..."

He shook his head, smiling. "I knew you would be worried about that. I have it on good authority my brother has some news to share with Beth tomorrow. A new job and a new address are in her future if she wants it." He leaned his forehead to mine. "Say yes, baby."

A car went by and honked, and Liam glared as they drove past. I had to laugh. "Maybe we should go inside and talk."

He shook his head. "This is our spot. It's like lunch. Only ours. All of our big conversations have happened here."

"I have to talk to Beth. I-I can't leave her behind, Liam."

He smiled. "I love your open, giving heart, Paige. I adore the fact that you're worried about Beth, and Ronan thinks she'll have the same reaction. We know how close you are." He ran his finger down my cheek. "So, if she says yes, then you'll say yes?"

"Yes."

He bent low and kissed me. "Then it's as good as a done deal. I get you and Lucy. Ronan gets Beth and Evan. It's perfect."

CHAPTER SIXTEEN

LIAM

Sunday night, the four of us sat together and figured things out. The girls were thrilled for each other, hugging and talking quietly. I shook Ronan's hand and clapped his shoulder.

"Onward and upward, little bro."

I looked at Paige, sitting across from me. "When is your lease up?"

"Not until November, but I called the landlord today. He told me he just had a family member asking about the place. He said he'd let us out of the lease at the end of August." She looked doubtful. "It's pretty fast, though. That's only six weeks away."

Ronan and I shook our heads. "Totally doable," he disagreed. "Mom and Dad are gonna have Evan for a while so Dad can work one-on-one with him on his leg. We can move his stuff to my place right away, and he can just stay there. We'll hire movers for your stuff. You won't have to worry about it."

"I'll have Lucy's room done by the team. I can have your part of the office set up fast, Paige," I added. "A desk and a chair and whatever else you need."

Beth and Paige glanced at each other. "What?" I asked.

Paige smiled, covering my hand. "Most of the furniture is pieces we bought second- or thirdhand. Aside from some things that belonged to Beth's parents, and the kids' and our personal stuff, there isn't a lot we want to bring from here."

I squeezed her fingers. "Whatever you want is fine. Leave it for the next people, or we'll haul it away. But we both have lots of space. Bring anything you want."

"We have extra storage space at the Hub. Each family gets a section," Ronan said. "You don't have to leave anything behind you want to keep."

The next day after dinner, I took Lucy and Paige for ice cream. Lucy scrambled onto my lap as always, often requesting help when her ice cream dripped. After I licked the ice cream for her, I touched her nose. "So, Munchkin, I want to ask you something."

"Otay," she replied, busy with her cone.

"How would you feel about you and your momma coming to live with me?"

She stopped, staring up at me. "By the water? In your house?"

"Yes."

"With your daddy and mommy? Ava?"

"Yes."

She hesitated then, looking sad, shook her head. "No."

I met Paige's startled gaze over Lucy's head.

"Why not, Lucy-loo?" she asked calmly.

"I miss Evan too much."

I grinned. "Then you'll be happy to know that Evan is moving too."

"Oh! With us?"

"He'll live with Beth and Ronan," Paige explained patiently. "You'll see him all the time."

"Can I bring my unicorn?"

"You can bring all your stuff. Anything you want."

She held up her cone, and I caught the drips and returned it. She licked in silence, a thoughtful expression on her face.

She crooked her finger, and I lowered my head. She cupped my ear. "Can I call you Daddy, then?" she whispered.

I lifted my head, meeting Paige's tear-filled eyes.

"Soon, Munchkin. I promise you soon."

"Otay," she replied happily. "I say yes, then."

Well, that was settled.

Somehow, the days got busier, yet time seemed to stand still. I couldn't wait for Lucy and Paige to move in with me. Beth and Evan were moving out first, and I planned on staying with Paige and Lucy in the house until my home was totally ready. Not only was I having Lucy's room done, but I was redoing the office so

Paige had a comfortable place to work, and I was having the place painted. I had Paige sit with Liv to choose colors, and I asked Liv to encourage Paige to pick a few items she liked for the various rooms. I wanted her to feel as if she belonged in the house, not simply moving in to my space. As soon as it was ready, I planned on bringing Lucy and Paige out to the house and handing her keys back to the landlord. The rent was already paid up, and he could let his nephew move in whenever he wanted.

I should be excited and looking forward to the new direction my life had taken, yet something kept holding me back.

The answer became clear as Paige stood in Lucy's almost complete room, looking in wonder at the bookcase Van had brought over. He had made it years ago when Sammy was a little girl. It was like a castle and went with the theme of the room. Sammy had been happy to loan it to Lucy for a few years.

Paige ran her fingers over the wood. "He spent a lot of time on this."

"A labor of love."

"He gave it to Sammy when he and Liv were dating?"

"Yes."

"He must have already loved them."

I crossed my arms. "I think so. He's a straight shooter. I know they went through a lot when Sammy was little. Her father tried to take her away, and Van fought alongside Liv to make sure it didn't happen."

She met my eyes. "You'd do the same."

"I would do anything for you and Lucy," I said. "You're my entire world."

Right then, I knew what I wanted.

"Lucy wants to call me Daddy."

She smiled softly. "I know."

I walked toward her, taking her hand. "I want her to. I want her to belong to me. I want you both to belong to me."

"I think we do since we're moving in with you."

I shook my head. "It's not enough."

"Not enough?"

"No, I want the world to know. I want to adopt Lucy. I want—" I paused and swallowed "—I want to marry you."

PAIGE

My head swirled with Liam's words. I blinked at him, unsure how to respond. He cupped my cheek. "I know I just shocked you, Sweet Pea, but it's the truth. I want to marry you. I want to adopt Lucy and be a real family. I want you to have my name, and I want Lucy to have it as well."

"Liam," I whispered. "Are you sure? We might get here and drive you crazy. You might wish—"

He cut me off with a laugh. "Don't even go there. I am not going to change my mind. Nothing you could do would make me change my mind." He slid his arm around my waist. "Don't you feel how right we are, baby? You, me, and Lucy? We're so good together." He pressed a kiss to my cheek. "Even if that is all we have, it is enough."

I met his earnest gaze. He meant it. He wouldn't push me for more—ever. I cupped his face, his dear, wonderful face, and smiled.

"No, it's not, Liam."

His grip tightened. "What are you saying?"

"If we go forward, I want to give it all to you. The chance for children of your own. You're right. We'd love them together, no matter what. I want to give you everything."

"If?" he asked, his voice gruff. "You're not sure?"

"Is there a big hurry?"

"Yes. I want to marry you as soon as possible. Before you move in. I want to take this next step of our journey as husband and wife. And daughter. In this house."

"That's only a couple of weeks away," I protested.

"Do you want a big wedding? The church, the dinner, all the trappings?"

"Lord no, but your family—"

He shook his head. "Our marriage is private. It's us. We'll get married quietly. My family can throw a party after. They'd love that."

"I-I don't know what to say."

He clutched me to him. "Say yes, baby. Say yes to a lifetime with me."

"I have to think. I—"

He cut me off with a kiss. "You think. I'll plan. I promise you we'll be great together, Paige. Life will be good with me."

I smiled. "It already is, Liam."

Beth's eyes were wide when I told her what Liam wanted.

I plucked at the edge of my shirt in nervousness. "And he wants to do it soon. Before I move in."

"And you don't? Too fast?" she asked, concerned.

I sighed. "That's the scary part, Beth. I do. I want to marry him. I want to let Lucy call him Daddy. She's dying to do so." I laughed softly. "So is he, I think."

"But…"

"Shouldn't I be scared? After what happened before? Shouldn't all this scare the shit out of me? I mean, is there something wrong with me that all I can think of is how much I want that too?"

The questions kept playing over in my mind.

Beth took my hand. "Some people would think so, but I don't. Liam is different. I've seen how he looks at you. The love he feels for you and Lucy. He's like Ronan. What you see is what you get. They're special. Wonderful. And you love him, don't you?"

"I do. I know he's nothing like my ex. You would just think I would want to be more cautious."

"Or maybe your heart knows what is right. You said you had doubts last time. Do you feel those with Liam?"

"None. All I feel is an absolute rightness."

"Then say yes."

I wanted to. I had sat up most of the night thinking about it.

"Neither of us wants a big wedding. In fact, we only plan on getting married with our witnesses. Maybe a party after if anyone was interested?"

Beth laughed. "As if this family would let an occasion like that go without a party?"

I sniffled. "Our family," I said softly and flung my arms around her neck. "Now we get to be real sisters."

She hugged me, her voice happy. "Yes, we do."

Liam was quieter than normal when he arrived for lunch on Monday. He brought me a small bunch of flowers, not an unusual thing anymore, but I knew there was more to the gesture than simply making me happy.

I took them from his hands, inhaling the sweet perfume. He always included my favorites, and today's bouquet was rich with the scent of lilies and tiny roses. I slipped them into a vase after thanking him.

We ate the sandwiches at the table, the bouquet sitting in the middle.

"So pretty," I murmured, stroking the petals. "Almost like a bridal bouquet."

The air around us buzzed with sudden tension.

He lifted his eyebrows, his voice low. "You think so?"

I met his gaze, intense and yet hopeful. I knew he'd been holding back, not saying a word since his impromptu proposal on Saturday. But Beth was correct. I felt the rightness of us. The belief in our future. Liam was it for me. He wanted this.

I wanted this.

"*Yes.*"

He knew I was answering his proposal. He was out of his chair and I was in his arms in seconds. He kissed me hard, holding me tight.

"I love you," he repeated over and again. "Life is going to be amazing. I promise."

I held him close.

"I know."

Beth grinned at me. "Nervous?"

I fluffed the skirt of my dress. I was wearing the one Cami had given me, the sleeve repaired and perfect. Liam loved it, and I wanted the memory of my wearing it today to be the one he thought of. I held a small bouquet of roses and sweet peas—how Liam found them this late into the season, I didn't know, but he had.

"No," I answered truthfully.

"Good."

Liam stepped into the room, Lucy in his arms. She wore a pretty dress I had bought her and carried a matching bouquet. Beth had one as well, and Liam, Ronan, and Evan each had a small rose pinned to their lapel.

"The justice is ready for us." He held out his hand. "Okay?"

I slid my hand into his, his grip strong and steady. I looked into his eyes.

"Okay."

The service was quick and simple. We said I do, repeated vows, and signed a piece of paper. Ronan used his phone and took a lot of pictures. When the justice of the peace pronounced us husband and wife, Lucy had piped up, exclaiming gleefully, "And me!"

Liam kissed me leisurely and thoroughly, whispering words of love against my mouth. Then he bent and scooped Lucy up and kissed her cheek. "And you, Munchkin."

She cupped her hand, and he leaned close, a smile breaking out on his face at her whispered query. He nodded, and she smiled in return, the sunshine of her happiness making us all smile.

"I love you, Daddy."

He wrapped his arm around me, drawing me into their love fest.

"My girls," he said. "All mine."

Ronan clapped and Beth beamed, her eyes misty. I knew she wouldn't be far behind me, although I had a feeling she wanted a bigger wedding. All I wanted was Liam.

Evan took a picture and nodded. "Good one."

Liam took the camera and studied it. Evan had captured his wide smile, Lucy in one arm and me tucked against him in the other.

"Yes," he agreed. "Perfect."

CHAPTER SEVENTEEN
LIAM

"**Y**ou ready to do this?" I asked Paige.

My new wife sat in the passenger seat of the truck. We'd had two days and three nights of just us. A hotel, a big bathtub, room service, and her naked most of the time. It had been a perfect way to start off our married life.

While we were rolling around in a hotel suite, unbeknownst to her, my brother and Beth moved the last of Paige's things into the house and returned the keys to the landlord. Paige would never have to go back or be alone again. I planned to tell her later, but for now, we had some other news to share.

"Maybe we could put it off."

I laughed and lifted her hand to my mouth, kissing her knuckles. The light glinted off the diamonds on her hand. "The women are gonna spot the rock before you even say hello. The cat is going to be out of the bag fast. Best we confess and get ahead of the curve."

She regarded me, worried. "Will they be upset?"

"My mom and dad eloped. I think they'll understand. Besides, they'll throw a party, and everything will be fine."

She blew out a breath. "Okay, let's do this."

"That's my girl."

We entered the Hub, glad to see we had arrived before Beth and Ronan. I was certain Lucy would spill the beans before we had a chance to share our news. My parents were at the table, the coffeepot in the middle. Bentley and Emmy, Maddox and Dee, plus Nan and Pops were there.

We joined them, Paige sitting down quickly. I laughed under my breath when I noticed she had her hand tucked under the pretty skirt she wore today.

"How was your break?" Bentley asked.

Dad laughed. "You two look pretty tired, so I'd say it was good."

Mom slapped his shoulder. "Aiden," she admonished.

"Just saying."

I shook my head. Leave it to my dad to say something inappropriate. I cleared my throat. "It was good. We, ah, have some news to share."

Mom smiled. "Oh?"

I tugged Paige's hand from its hiding spot. "We got married."

For a moment, everyone stared at the ring on Paige's finger. The thick band on mine. Then Maddox spoke.

"You owe me a hundred bucks, Aiden."

"Me too," Bentley said, taking a sip of his coffee.

"You bet on me getting married?" I asked.

Maddox grinned. "You never take a break. To suddenly disappear with Paige? I saw Lucy with Ronan, so I figured the jig was up. You're too much like your father not to. He said you wouldn't. It was a wager we couldn't pass up."

"I didn't think you'd get married without at least telling your mother," Aiden pouted.

Cami laughed. "Love always wins, Aiden. I was in on that bet. You owe me too."

A huge smile broke out on his face. "I'm happy to pay up on this one."

Suddenly, everyone was on their feet. There were hugs and kisses. Laughter. A few tears. Paige's ring was admired. My shoulder was clasped and shaken. My mom wept. So did Paige. Nan beamed, and I bent low to accept her congratulations.

"She is perfect for you," she told me.

"I know."

Ronan walked in with Beth, Lucy streaking past them. "Momma! Daddy! I missed you!"

I scooped her up, and she kissed all over my face as if it had been years, not a couple of days. She did the same to Paige, then proceeded to detail all the things they did while we were gone. The zoo and the park. The pizza. So many things to tell us about.

I sat down, and my dad leaned over. "That's why Ronan had her. So we wouldn't find out. I assume he was at your wedding?"

"We wanted it private, Dad. It was an important day to us. It was *just* for us." I stressed.

"I get it. We're thrilled for you. But you won't deny your family a chance to celebrate, will you?"

"No, in fact, we're counting on it."

He whooped. "Party time in the compound." Then he swung Lucy into his arms. "And I think, young lady, it's time you called me Pops."

She frowned and pointed at Jordan. "That's Pops." Then her face smoothed out. "You're PopPop." She grinned at Cami. "You're Grammy."

Cami kissed her hand. "Perfect." She looked at Evan. "You better do the same thing."

He grinned. "Okay."

Lucy reached for me. "This is my daddy."

The room gave a collective *"ah"* as I wrapped my arms around her. "That's right, Munchkin. I'm your daddy."

I met Paige's eyes and leaned close, kissing her. I pressed my lips to her ear.

"I'll be your daddy too if you want. Just like last night."

She laughed and shook her head.

"You're incorrigible."

I winked.

I'd be anything she wanted.

Always.

———

A week later, we were back at the Hub.

The noise level was high, the laughter constant, and everywhere I looked, there were people.

My family. *Our* family now.

I tightened my arm around Paige's waist and looked down with a grin.

"Regretting this?"

She squeezed my hip. "No."

"Good. Because it's just getting started."

It was a glorious evening at the compound. The perfect sort of night—the type where summer started losing its grip, yet autumn hadn't stepped in. The breeze was cool, but the sun still sat high in the sky. The doors to the Hub were wide open, the huge deck strung with lights. Music played, and I knew there were two fire pits ready to light on the beach. Inside the building, tables groaned with food, and the furniture was pushed back for dancing. News of our marriage had spread fast, and the house had buzzed with visitors dropping in every day to wish us well. And tonight, we would celebrate.

"Daddy?"

My heart did a strange little thump every time Lucy said that word. I loved hearing it.

"Yeah, Munchkin?" I said, turning to meet her gaze. She sat in the crook of my arm, one of her favorite ways to travel.

She cupped her hand close to my ear. "Can I eats lots of cake today?"

I saw Paige's lips quirk. Lucy still didn't quite get the whispering part of secrets at times. Luckily, "lots" to her was a bite or two before she got distracted when there was a large group. She left a trail of partially eaten tidbits everywhere she went. My job was usually to clean them up. I had been working out a lot more these days thanks to that endeavor.

"You can eat whatever you want tonight."

"Maybe I take home a piece for Mr. Teddy and Fluffy?"

Her favorite stuffed animals were waiting at home for her on her bed. Her reaction to her new room had been nothing short of spectacular. She hadn't known where to look, what to touch, or how to respond when she first saw it. Liv had done an amazing job. The entire room was pink and cream, with lots of flowery fabric, lace, and forgiving edges. The bed was a masterpiece of girlie-ness, and Liv and Paige had added tiny lights to the fabric that draped over the top of the bed. At night, their soft glow fascinated Lucy. The whole room did, and every time she disappeared during the first week, we knew where to find her.

"I bet they would love that," I assured her. "Grammy will make sure to save them a piece if you ask her."

Lucy smiled wide, then her eyes grew round. "Oh! There's PopPop!" She pushed on my chest, hurrying toward Dad, who bent low, opening his arms. He doted on her, and aside from me and Ronan, he was her favorite Callaghan man.

I banded my arm around Paige again. "What about you, Momma? You want to eat a lot of cake tonight?"

She rolled her eyes. "Duh. It's cake. Beth made it, so of course I'm going to eat it."

I pulled her close as we headed toward the group of people waiting for us. "Then let's get at it."

An hour later, my shoulder ached from all the slaps, and I had been hugged more times than I could count. Neither Paige nor I could take more than a couple of steps without being stopped, congratulated, and handed a fresh drink, some food, or, at the very least, advice. Some of it, from my idiot brothers, I planned to ignore, but everyone was well-meaning and happy for us. There had been no discord over the fact that we had eloped. As long as my family got to celebrate in some sort of fashion, they were good with it.

Ronan had printed some of the pictures he had snapped with his phone and had given us copies of them all. One, in particular, was my favorite, and my mom had blown it up for tonight. Paige was tucked into my side, beautiful and smiling, Lucy in my other arm, her little face beaming, and I looked as if I had just won the lottery. Which I had—I got the two of them. That picture was framed on the table stacked with gifts for us to open. We had requested no presents, but I was pleased to notice many of them were addressed to Lucy and Paige. The packages were to welcome them to the family. It warmed my heart how they had been accepted.

My parents had already given us a gift. They were sending us on a Disney cruise and a three-day stay at the park. I'd thought Lucy was going to fall off my knee in excitement when she realized what the gift was. The best part was when Mom informed us she and my dad were coming along.

"We're sharing a room with Lucy. You and Paige have your own suite," she said quietly. "Ronan and Beth are coming as well. They have their own suite with Evan. Family during the day. Your honeymoon at night." She smiled. "We couldn't exclude Evan."

I had to admit, my first thought had been how much Evan would love to go. My parents' thoughtful gesture touched both Paige and me. We shared a glance, knowing how much this would mean to him.

Dad leaned close. "I've arranged for a scooter for Evan at the park. He can get around easier and do more. I talked to him, and he agreed it was fine. It's all taken care of."

"Thanks, Dad."

Paige hugged him and Mom, wiping the tears off her face at their generosity.

Dad grinned. "Lucy, Evan, and I are gonna have a blast! We'll sit down and map it all out."

Her squeal said it all.

Paige was overwhelmed. "I've never been outside Canada," she confessed.

I kissed her. "The first of many trips, I promise."

Paige turned away to talk to Nan, and I headed to the bar to get a fresh drink. No matter how many I had been handed, I kept losing them when someone would swoop in for a hug. I was parched from all the talking. I poured a splash of vodka into the glass and topped it with tonic and lots of ice. I turned and surveyed the place, unable to stop my smile. The elders of BAM gathered together as they usually did. Bentley, Dad, and Maddox were always easy to spot in this group. Richard and Katy had flown in, and he stood beside Maddox, laughing at something

Dad had just said. Nan and Pops sat together on the sofa, smiling and visiting. They were both a bit frailer now, but still going strong. They ceded to sitting more and allowed us to "run and fetch" when they wanted something, but otherwise, they acted younger than their years. I spotted Van close to my dad, talking to Hal and Reid, the three of them in an intense conversation. Groupings of siblings and cousins were everywhere. Jaxson already had Gracie dancing, his arms holding her close. Brayden and Addi were headed to the center of the room to join them. I caught my mom's eye and smiled. She was with Emmy, Dee, Liv, Fiona, Becca, and Katy. Lucy was on her knee, entertaining them. The cluster of women—the real strength behind the family—and the very nucleus of all the men I admired. They made this place a home, these gatherings a joy, and I was grateful for each one of them.

Halton spotted me and broke away from Van and Reid. He shook my hand with a wry grin. "How you doing?"

I sipped my drink. "Great."

"Awesome party as usual."

"It is."

"I wanted you to know, I put forth your adoption petition yesterday. It's all complete and filed. I expect zero problems with it."

"Awesome."

Hal grinned. "You're as anxious as Van was when he adopted Sammy. Lucy is already yours in every way that counts."

"I know. I want her to have my name, though. I want her to know she belongs to this family. To me. I never want her to doubt how much I love her."

Hal squeezed my shoulder. "She does. I've never seen a happier child. She's pure sunshine."

"She is."

"You know, given what I did for a living, I never wanted to get married," he mused. "I never understood the meaning of family." He snorted. "I certainly never wanted children."

I met his eyes with a grin. "Have you checked lately? You have five, Halton." I stated dryly.

His laughter was loud. "I am aware. But it was Fiona who changed all that. Meeting your family, being drawn into them, changed *me*. I saw what a real family could be. How it could complete a person." He paused, sipping his drink. "My kids—my family—mean the world to me. They are my greatest treasure." He grinned. "Most of the time anyway. I admit there were a few times I would have liked to bury one or two of them."

We both laughed.

"Fiona taught me all I had to do was love them. That was all they really needed. You do that for Lucy. I see it. Everyone does." He clapped my shoulder again. "She is going to be fine. You all are." Then he winked. "Talk to me in a few years about how many kids I have. I get the feeling you and your siblings are going to keep your parents pretty busy with grandbabies."

Chuckling, he walked away.

A few other people found me, and we chatted before they drifted away. It was always good to catch up with those I didn't see on a regular basis. I cast my gaze around the room, looking for Paige. She'd seemed quite nervous over tonight's party. I wasn't sure if it was the thought of how many of us there would be, the fact that she'd be the center of their attention, or if she was reacting to something else. She'd been quiet most of the day, but I had chalked it up to nerves. Maybe it was more. She'd certainly tried to hide it. I hadn't planned on leaving her side tonight but, given this group, wasn't shocked to find us pulled in different directions. I wanted to check on her, but she didn't seem to be in the main room.

Movement caught my eye, and I saw a solitary figure heading down the steps to the beach. I knew where I would find my wife —on the sand, close to the fire, staring at the stars.

Setting down my drink, I followed her.

PAIGE

I slipped out the side door, to a quiet part of the deck. It led to a staircase to the beach, and I made my way to the sand, the torches lighting my path. I turned and looked at the brightly lit building behind me. I could hear the laughter, the sounds of music. I breathed in the scent of the water, the low-burning fire, and the sand. I wondered if I would ever get used to this spot. The ever-changing beauty of it. The lovely place that felt like home already—because Liam was there.

I loved the house. The big windows, the large porch. Liam had put my desk in front of the window, and as I worked, I could look outside and see the trees and water—unlike my desk in Toronto, where I stared at my neighbor's side door and driveway. My life had taken on a new rhythm, and every day I sank more into the gentle cadence of it. Lucy was so happy and settled, taking to the new surroundings like a duck to water. With Beth and Evan close, and encircled by Liam's family, she'd never been happier.

My family now, too. It still seemed unreal. All of this seemed unreal at times. I was certain I would wake up and find I had been dreaming.

Only a few months ago, I was struggling to make sure we stayed on a tight budget. I worked as many hours as possible, even pulling some of the night shifts to add a little to the bank account. I spent the rest of the time looking after Lucy and Evan, always grateful to have Beth and Evan in our life. We created our own little family, and together, we managed to get by. I would never have made it without Beth. I would never have met Liam without her either.

He was incredible. There was no other word to describe him. His love enfolded us on a daily basis. I felt stronger because of him. His affection was offered freely and openly. He gave me security I had never known, both emotionally and financially. I was still getting used to both. I hoped never to take either for granted.

I startled as a strong arm wrapped around my waist, and I was pulled back to a warm chest.

"Hiding, Sweet Pea? Our family too much?"

The easy use of his phrase "our family" made tears come to my eyes. I patted his arm. "No. But the draw of the fire was too much."

He chuckled. "I figured."

He sat down on one of the logs placed around the pit. It had been smoothed out over the years of use, the wood faded from the sun. He reached into a basket and pulled out a blanket. Opening his legs, he put it on the sand and patted his knee.

"Come here, Sweet Pea."

I nestled between his legs, copying the way we had always sat on the steps in Toronto. It was our thing when we needed to talk.

Liam waited, always patient. He stroked my neck, his touch light.

"Whatever you're thinking, Paige, you can tell me. I'm here."

I found his hand and kissed the palm, holding it to my cheek. "I know."

"Are you unhappy, baby?"

"Oh God, no." I lifted my face to meet his eyes. "I've never been happier."

"Good. Me too. But something is on your mind."

I drew in a deep breath. "I saw my new doctor yesterday."

"You didn't tell me." His hand stilled. "Is something wrong?"

"No. I'm perfectly healthy."

"Okay. But?"

"She wants me off the birth control pills."

"Good. I read about the side effects, and they're scary." He paused. "I'll get condoms. Let me take the responsibility off you."

I turned, playing with his fingers, spinning his thick band around over and again.

"What if-what if we didn't use any birth control?"

His breath stuttered, and his body locked down. "Are you saying what I think you're saying?"

"I want to try for a baby with you." I swallowed. "If you want. I mean, if you're ready. I know it's sudden—"

He cut off the rest of my words, his mouth covering mine. He pulled me off the sand and onto his lap, never stopping the sweet possession of his lips.

Finally, he pulled back, resting his forehead to mine. "Really?"

"Yes. I want to try. You were right—things are different. I have you. Our family. Whatever we have to face, we'll face it together."

He cupped my cheek and kissed my forehead, his lips lingering. "Thank you. This is the best gift I've ever been given."

"It might take a while. Dr. Carter warned me about that."

"I'm up for the challenge," he assured me, his voice low.

"I'm not surprised."

"In fact, everyone is busy. Let's sneak home, and I'll show you just how up for it I am."

I laughed, the sound drifting across the sand.

"I don't think we can leave our own party to go try to make babies."

"I would argue differently. It's the perfect time. Lucy's occupied, the house is empty. My cock is on board..." He trailed off, joining in my laughter.

"Okay." He relented. "But I'm getting Mom and Dad to keep Lucy tonight. I want you loud and vocal while we start this endeavor." He sighed against my hair. "It's gonna be a tough job, but I'll give it my best shot."

I hummed, nestling closer. "I love you, Liam."

He tightened his arms. "I love you, Sweet Pea. Always."

EPILOGUE
LIAM

FIVE YEARS LATER...

I woke, my hand automatically searching for Paige. Not only was I surprised to find the bed empty but the sun already high in the sky. Normally I was the first one awake in the house, even beating my girls, who were early risers.

I flung back the blanket and stood, stretching out my back. I grimaced at the grip of still-aching muscles. We had installed a massive garden the past couple of days, working well into the evening to get it done for the client. I wasn't as involved in the physical side of the business anymore, and the twinge in my back reminded me why.

Once Paige and I were married and settled in Port Albany, I hired more staff and limited myself to the overseeing and design. I hired another landscape architect once our first baby was born to help manage my time. Joanna worked primarily in Toronto, and I concentrated on the outlying areas. It freed up a lot of commute time, which meant I got to spend it with my family.

When a second baby came along rather quickly, I depended more on Joanna than ever. We did a lot of meetings via phone, and we shared travel, her coming this way on occasion and me heading into Toronto at other times. The truth was, I hated missing a minute of my babies growing up.

Dr. Carter had warned us it could take a while for Paige to get pregnant. It happened almost immediately. I came home from work to find her sitting on the floor of our bathroom, a stick in her hand, her expression shocked.

I crouched beside her. "Sweet Pea? What is it?"

"I don't know what fertilizer you use, Liam, but holy shit," she whispered, showing me the two blue lines.

I was ecstatic. I scooped her into my arms, holding her tight. I felt the tension in her body, the worry already taking hold. I pressed a kiss to her head. "Together, baby. We'll handle it together."

Lucy had been excited when we told her she was going to have a sibling. Her eyes got big in her face, and she hugged Mr. Teddy close.

"Will the baby share my room?"

I lifted her to my knee. "Nope. That is yours. I am going to make the baby a room."

"Can I play with her?"

"Well, we don't know yet if it's a her or a him, and they'll be pretty small, but you can help Momma. And once the baby is bigger, I'm sure they'd love to play with you."

She nodded, happy, hugging Mr. Teddy. "It's a girl. I know it."

And she was right.

The day Shannon was born was one of the most amazing days of my life. Seeing Paige give birth was awe-inspiring. I had always known how strong she was, but that day, she was incredible. I was nervous and anxious, fumbling in my attempts to be helpful. She was calm and settled, only breaking down when Shannon was born, healthy and strong, all limbs intact. Even though the ultrasounds had shown no problems, I knew she worried. I held her as she wept in my arms when we were alone, letting her cry out the last nine months of secret apprehension.

"Let it out, Sweet Pea. Then we can move forward with all the good things." I tucked her closer. "I need you to show me how to be a good dad."

"You already are a good dad."

"I've never had a baby before. Lucy came toilet trained and walking. She could even feed herself." I teased. "This little bundle seems a bit uncoordinated."

That made her laugh, the humor breaking her tension. She wiped her face and sat up. "You'll be amazing at being a new daddy." She let out a stuttering breath. "And this time, I get to enjoy it more."

That led to another round of sobs, which I understood. I knew how alone and scared she'd been when Lucy was born. The lack of sleep, trying to work and look after a newborn all on her own took a toll.

But this time, she had me. My family. I had finally convinced her to give up her job. She'd enjoyed the latter part of her pregnancy, no longer worrying about money or bills. She concentrated on the house, Lucy, and me. And, for the first time ever, herself.

When she discovered she was pregnant again, her fears were lower. The tests showed everything was good, and she let it go.

I now had three daughters. Lucy, Shannon, and Erin. I was surrounded by all things girl. I felt sometimes as if I lived in a perpetual state of glitter and pink. Yet, I wouldn't trade it for the world.

Squeals of laughter brought me out of my musings, and I went to the window, grinning at the sight that met my eyes.

My girls were in the back, dogpiling on my dad, who was laughing as loudly as they were. I saw Mom sitting under the gazebo. I hurried and got washed and dressed to go and join them.

I walked through the house, the changes in the place reflected everywhere. Some subtle, others very obvious. When I'd drawn up the plans for the house originally, I'd had it built to be able to add a second story if needed. Once Paige was pregnant, I put that plan into action, adding the addition with three bedrooms and a large bath. Lucy's room was now up there, and Shannon was across the hall from her. Erin was still too little for the stairs, but eventually, she would move upstairs as well. I still had my office I shared with Paige, and once Erin was settled upstairs, we would have a guest room again. The rest of the house looked much the same, except for Paige's touches. She added a softer element to the rooms. Warmer colors on the walls, toss cushions, thick, warm rugs underfoot on the hardwood floor. Lots of family photos. There were also endless toys, hair ribbons, bows, and little shoes everywhere that I constantly picked up.

I headed outside, grinning as the girls spotted me and deserted my dad. I was crushed in a mass of arms, smiles, and curls as my girls greeted me as if they hadn't seen me for weeks instead of yesterday at breakfast.

I kissed Shannon's cheek, her hazel eyes twinkling. "How was dance class?"

"I got a part in the recital!"

"Oh yeah?"

"I'm a dancing tree!"

"Awesome, my little ballerina. You'll be the best tree ever." She loved to dance, although she wasn't very coordinated. We encouraged her, nonetheless, and would be there to applaud her waving of her twigs or whatever a dancing tree did on stage.

"Munchkin, how's the arm?" I asked Lucy. She'd been fitted with a prosthetic recently that was pretty amazing. The fingers moved and bent, and it looked realistic. The wrist flexed. She had finally decided she wanted to try one, and I had been all too happy to encourage it. It would have to be replaced as she grew, but I was pleased she wanted to try. At ten, she was growing so fast. We were best buds, and I adored her. She was smart and funny and still looked so much like me, it was uncanny. No one thought she was anything but my biological daughter, and I rarely disabused them of that idea. She simply was my daughter, no matter what sperm had created her.

"Daddy," she said, her eyes sparkling. "I caught a ball yesterday." She held up her arm. "With Robby."

I grinned and high-fived "Robby." She had nicknamed her arm. "Awesome."

I lifted Erin, kissing her chubby little cheek. She was tiny and sweet. The quietest of the bunch. She looked like Paige, with her dark hair and blue eyes. "How's my little bee?"

She buzzed everywhere. She was always in the garden around the flowers, happiest when digging and planting. In the house, she had a window garden I'd made for her that she tended daily. She'd been two when she discovered plants, and since then, I couldn't keep her away from them, not that I tried hard. At three, she loved everything about flowers and was with me as often as possible when I worked around the grounds.

"Good," she lisped. "Momma bots me new flowas. You hep me?"

I bit back my laughter. No doubt they'd been in town and Erin had spotted some pretty flowers she had to have. Or half-dead ones she wanted to "fix." Paige rarely said no to buying her plants—no matter their condition.

"Yes, Daddy will help. I'm gonna have coffee with Grammy, and then we'll plant them, okay?"

"Otay."

"Go back to PopPop."

I high-fived my dad and headed to Mom. I kissed her cheek and sat down, accepting the cup of coffee she offered me. "Where's Paige?"

"She had errands. She asked us to sit with the girls. She said you'd worked late the last couple of nights and were exhausted."

I grinned. "And sore. I'm not used to it anymore. But it's done, the building opens today, and the grounds look spectacular. Joanna is going to send me some pics today when she's there." I yawned. "Paige let me sleep in. I don't usually do that."

"You needed it." Mom smiled.

"Guess so. How long has Paige been gone?"

"She'll be home soon."

"What kinds of errands?"

Mom shrugged. "Ones she had to do. I didn't ask." She smirked. "She'll be home soon, Liam."

The sound of an engine coming close filled the air. "There she is. Go help her with the bags, and I'll go make the girls a snack. Your father will be hungry too."

I laughed as I headed to the front of the house. Paige sat behind the wheel of the SUV I had bought her. She looked contemplative but waved when she saw me. I opened her door and she slipped out. I kissed her hello, smiling against her mouth. "Hey, Sweet Pea."

"Hi."

I opened the trunk, surprised to see no bags. I checked the back seat, but it was empty. "Didn't find what you were looking for?"

"What?"

"Mom said you had errands. I assumed the grocery store or some other place that involved bags."

"No," she said, distracted. She stood still, not moving toward the house. Her fingers fidgeted with the strap of her purse, a sure indication she was nervous. Something was up. I could feel it.

"Paige."

"Hmm?"

"Where were you?"

She frowned. "What?"

I stepped closer, cupping her face. "What's going on?"

She sighed and leaned into my touch.

"Baby, you're scaring me a little," I confessed. "You seem out of sorts."

"No," she whispered. "Not out of sorts. Shocked."

"Shocked? By what?"

She lifted my free hand and pressed it to her stomach. "Your damn fertilizer worked again."

I blinked. Looked down. Glanced up. Looked down again. After Erin was born three years ago, we tried for a fourth. Nothing happened. After a while, we decided we had three healthy girls and should be content, so we let it go. Was Paige saying what I thought she was saying?

"You're pregnant?"

She nodded. "I thought I was gaining weight. I thought I was having my period at first, but that wasn't what it was. Then we've been so busy, I forgot. I'm almost three months along, Liam."

"Three months?" I repeated. "Is—Are you… Is everything okay?"

She pressed a small black-and-white picture into my hand. "Everything is okay. It was a little spotting, but Dr. Carter says everything looks fine."

I peered at the image, the small bean in the center. My child. Our child. We were going to have another baby.

I lifted Paige in my arms, holding her. I kissed her once. Twice. A third time. "A baby," I said in wonder. Then I chuckled. "No guest room."

"Nope."

"I like this much better."

"Maybe it'll be a boy this time."

I shrugged. "If not, I'm good with my girls. I just want him or her healthy." I hugged her close. "Can we tell my parents?"

"Your mom already suspects. But your dad is clueless."

"Typical," I snorted. "Such amazing news, Sweet Pea. Thank you."

She smiled and snuggled close. "I think it was our weekend away."

"Ah. The B&B in Niagara." I pressed a kiss to her head. "I do remember your wandering hands on our picnic. I think we scared some wildlife that afternoon with your brazen behavior."

She slapped my chest. "It was your idea."

"I do have the best ones." I agreed. "Like choosing you as my wife."

The sound of running feet made me grin. "Brace yourself, Momma. Here come the girls. I wonder how they'll take to the news?"

"I guess we'll find out."

"I guess we will."

A FEW WEEKS LATER...

"What?" Paige gasped.

Dr. Carter smiled. "Yep. Twins." She studied the image. "I can tell you the sex if you want."

I stared at her, dumbfounded. Twins? We were having twins?

"You must be mistaken," I said. "It's a shadow, right? Ronan should be having twins. He's a triplet. I'm not."

The doctor laughed. "It doesn't work that way. That's not a shadow. There are two babies. And listen." She adjusted a dial. "Two heartbeats."

The rapid noises filled my ears, and as I listened, I was able to detect two separate beats.

I looked at Paige. "Twins."

She nodded, her eyes filled with tears.

I leaned over and kissed her. "You want to know?"

We had known with the other two. We liked to be prepared.

"Yes."

"Hit us, Doc."

"You have two sons. Two healthy sons. Congratulations."

I kissed Paige again. "Two boys. *Holy shit*, the girls are going to go nuts. The babies don't stand a chance. They'll be henpecked from the get-go."

She laughed, wiping her tears. "I think I'll let you tell them."

"Shannon will want to exchange them," I mused. "At least one. She's counting on another girl. Boys are just...*eww*."

"Erin might try to plant them." Paige grinned, wiping her stomach and sitting up once the doctor finished. She gave us some books to look at, answered some questions, handed us the printouts that showed very clearly there were two babies. She also admonished Paige gently.

"You need lots of rest. There are more risks with twins. It's different. I want to see you more, and we'll monitor you closely. You're young and healthy, but we want to keep you that way."

"I'll take good care of her. I'll get her help," I interjected.

She smiled at me. "I know you will, Liam. I'll see you both in a few weeks."

She left, and I looked at the pictures. "Twins."

"Boys," said Paige. "I know nothing about boys."

"Good thing you have me. I'm an expert."

"So's your mom."

I laughed. "Expert at boys and more than one baby at a time."

I helped her off the table. She was a little shaky, so I slipped my arms around her.

"Sons. We're having sons."

"Yep."

"Where are we gonna put them?"

Paige was quiet for a moment. "Erin will go upstairs soon. Her room will be the nursery, and eventually, we'll turn the office into another bedroom."

That idea made sense.

"I could turn the garage into a part office, I suppose. It's big enough."

"Good plan, Daddy."

"Okay, let's get you home, and I'll look into some help."

She was quiet on the car ride home. My thoughts were filled with the future. Baseball games in the summer, hockey on the ice during the winter with my boys. Them, my dad, and the other BAM men fishing. On the boat with Pops.

I had tried with the girls, but none of them was remotely interested in sports. Erin had wanted to try fishing with me, but she was horrified when I showed her how to hook a worm and had cried all the way home. I had to let her "free" the worms into her gardens to calm her. The next time I took her on the boat, we just sailed around in the water. My dad had laughed hard at that.

The only sport I was able to interest the girls in was skating, and I suspected it was more about the hot cocoa afterward than the actual skating, but I took what I could get.

Maybe now I could flex a little testosterone in the house. I wouldn't be so outnumbered.

This twin thing might work out well for me.

Later that night, I wandered the quiet house. I checked on all my girls.

Lucy had fallen asleep with music playing quietly in the background. Her room consisted of posters of her favorite singers and piles of clothes and books now. She still had her fairy bed, as she called it, but the rest of the room was more grown-up, although Mr. Teddy and Fluffy the unicorn were perched in places of honor. I shut off the music and stroked the hair off her forehead, bending down to brush a kiss to the smooth surface.

Across the hall, Shannon was asleep on the end of her bed, the blankets on the floor. She was restless at night, almost grudgingly giving in to sleep. I moved her back up to the pillows and draped the blanket back over her, knowing she'd end up on the bottom again before morning. I kissed her cheek, and she snuffled in her sleep at the touch of my beard on her skin. I left the nightlight on, the stars a dim glow on her ceiling.

Downstairs, Erin was a tight bundle in the middle of her bed. She never stopped all day long and crashed fast at night, barely moving until the morning. Her room was yellow and white, flowers everywhere on the fabric and wallpaper. She was wrapped around a stuffed penguin, her face buried in the black-and-white pelt. I brushed my hand over her soft hair, smiling at my youngest girl. She'd be up early with me tomorrow, anxious to see her flowers and the world.

I stood in our bedroom doorway, smiling at Paige. She was asleep early, her hand tucked under her cheek. She wore one of my T-shirts, liking the loose cotton on her skin. Her hand rested on her stomach, a bump already forming.

Our incredibly busy lives were about to change yet again. Two more babies would be added to our world. Two male babies in a house that had only ever known girl ones. Four girls, three boys.

All living under the same roof. Learning, growing, loving. I could imagine the mornings now. The craziness of dinnertime. The constant running to soccer practices, dance recitals, school functions. We were going to need a lot of help.

Life would be wild.

And I couldn't think of anything that would make me happier.

I slipped into bed, pulling Paige to my chest. She settled with a small noise, then she was out again.

I laid my hand over hers, knowing underneath them, our children slumbered.

All around me, my family was at rest. What a great future.

I closed my eyes and joined them. I was going to need the sleep.

Tomorrow beckoned.

TEN YEARS LATER…

LIAM

The phone rang and I sat up, startled and rubbing my eyes. I squinted at my watch, seeing it was just past midnight.

A phone call that late never boded well.

"Hello."

"Son, I thought you ought to know that AJ and Brock are in the pool. Again."

"What?" I let out a string of curse words. "How the hell did they get out of the house?"

"You'll have to ask them. They figured it out. Luckily, they didn't figure out the sensors I had put in around the pool. They went off, and I found the boys floating around like nothing was out of the ordinary."

"I'll be right there."

"Take your time. They're having fun."

"Fun?" I hissed. "It's midnight. They should be asleep." I hung up and flung back the covers.

"What now?" Paige asked, her voice dry.

I pulled on a pair of sweats. "Your sons found a way around the security system Reid put in, snuck out of the house, and are in the pool." I yanked a T-shirt over my head. "Again."

Paige sat up, wrapping her arms around her knees. "Why is it when they do these things, they're *my* sons? Other times, you claim ownership as well."

"Because right now, I want to lock them up and refuse to admit any of my DNA is inside them."

She burst out laughing. "Good luck with that. Your little mini-mes. They are the nine-year-old version of you, my darling husband."

"I think it's Reid's influence. Ronan's too."

She slipped back under the covers. "Okay. Have fun. Make sure to towel-dry their hair, or they'll get their pillows wet."

"You're not coming?"

She snuggled deeper. "Nope."

"Paige, we're supposed to be in this together."

"I'll withhold dessert. Make them do extra chores. I recall you gloating over having twin boys and how much of an expert you were at boys since you were one and all. You handle it."

I glared at her, then tugged the blanket over her shoulder and bent down and kissed her. "Once I'm finished dealing with our errant sons, I'm coming back to deal with my cheeky wife."

"Promises, promises."

I stomped to the pool, normally a five-minute walk. I did it in two. My dad was sitting on one of the chairs, dressed in sweats and a shirt like me. He had one ankle resting on his knee, leaning forward. "Put some muscle into it, AJ! Brock's beating you—again!" He sat back, grinning at me.

I sat beside him. "What are you doing?"

"Making them race each other until they're exhausted."

I sat back. "Good idea."

I watched them for a moment. "I have to punish them, Dad. What do I do?"

"What you think is best."

I snorted. "Thanks." I waved my hand. "They keep doing stuff! Sneaking out to the pool, stealing the golf cart, messing around on the rocks." I wiped my hand over my eyes. "Paige thinks it's a phase, but man, it's not ending. I got called to the school twice last week. Twice. The last week of school. Nothing should happen the last week of school."

"What did they do?"

I scrubbed my face. "One of their teachers pointed a ruler at a classmate and informed him at the end of the ruler was an idiot. They both yelled out, 'Which end?' Caused total chaos in the classroom. They got sent to the principal's office."

He guffawed, slapping his knee. "You have to admit that was a good one. What else?"

"They snuck into the principal's office and burped and farted into the loudspeaker."

"Did they get caught?"

"Not while doing it, but they laughed, and everyone knows their laugh. Even the principal. He called me."

They both laughed like braying donkeys—it was impossible to mistake.

"Amateurs," Dad snorted.

"It's not funny."

"It is because I'm not dealing with it."

I sat back with a groan. "It's my fault. I was over the moon when Paige was pregnant. Twin boys. I thought it would be great."

My dad turned in his chair. "Hey. They *are* great. They're well-behaved, smart, nice kids."

"Well-behaved?" I asked. "Did you just hear me about the school? Do you see the two delinquents in the pool at midnight?"

"They're no different than you or your brothers were at that age. The four of you used to get into trouble all the time."

"No, we didn't."

He scoffed at my words. "What about the time you threw manure over old man Tate's house in town? He'd just had it painted, and you four got into a manure fight right beside his house. The four of you stank for days. I had to pay to have the house cleaned and repainted."

"I remember having to do extra chores to pay you back."

He snorted. "You got off easy. Then there was the time you jumped off the cliffs when we were on vacation? Almost gave your mother a heart attack. Or the time Ronan switched out oil for soap in the bathrooms at school? Or Paul freed all the frogs in biology?"

I had forgotten those incidents.

"You and your brothers used to break out of your rooms on hot summer nights and come for a swim. You'd also get hungry and raid the refrigerator at the Hub and pass out there. By the third time we found you missing from your beds, we knew where to check."

"What about Ava?"

He shook his head. "She was the good one. The rest of you were little shits."

I laughed at his description. "These two make the girls look like angels."

Which they weren't, but they were far easier to deal with than the twins. I never knew what they were going to get up to. My dad was right, and they were nice boys. Friendly and well-liked, they stuck up for other kids, did well in school, and never went so far across the line it gave me pause. But they were full of mischievousness.

They'd been ahead of the curve their entire lives. The largest percentile for height and weight, they were off the charts. They were born early, and they walked early, literally crawling one day and on their feet the next. They communicated with each other in their own language before suddenly asking for something in plain English far too soon in their childhood. They went from babies to toddlers almost overnight. Walking, running, escaping. Their cribs were useless at holding them. The big-boy beds we bought barely kept them contained. Childproof locks were a joke. Splitting them up was a no-go. They would simply march into each other's room and crawl into the other's bed at some point after we said good night. Eventually, we gave up, and to this day, they shared a room. Erin never wanted to move upstairs, so instead we switched things around and the boys shared the largest room on the second floor.

At four, they pulled off pranks that drove their sisters crazy. By five, they were whiz kids on computers. By seven, they could take one apart and put it back together. AJ loved to write programs, the language coming easily to him. Brock loved to dismantle and improve machines. The office I had built in the garage was now filled with computer parts and machines. Reid loved spending time with them, amazed at their brilliance. He taught and encouraged them. It was the only time I ever saw them sit still and be quiet.

I thought of some of the scrapes they'd gotten into.

Experimenting with their mother's blender to make it "go faster."

We spent hours scrubbing cupboards, ceilings, and floors. The blender had to be thrown out when it burst into flames.

Deciding to find out what happens when you let the propane build up under the lid and then light the barbecue.

We changed to gas and added locks to the controls. It took three days until the lid washed up on shore, bent and barely recognizable. I replaced the scorched siding on the Hub and made the boys help repaint the trim.

Deciding to camp out overnight without telling us.

I had panicked and called my dad when I discovered the boys gone and their window open. He arrived with Bentley, Maddox, and Ronan, ready to start searching.

Bentley looked worried. "We should call the police."

Ronan looked out the window. "Maybe we should check over there."

I looked over his shoulder and saw the wisp of smoke in the trees. We found the boys stuffing their faces with marshmallows and looking shocked at our distress. They were calm and cool when I asked how they got out of their bedroom.

"We shimmied down the drainpipe, Dad. We tested it earlier when we took our supplies out."

I confiscated the pup tent and supplies, they were grounded, and I added sensors to the windows so they couldn't sneak out again. The drainpipe was moved.

Yet, they seemed to find ways around it.

"The point is, they're boys," Dad said. "I agree with Paige. This is a phase. You grew out of it, so will they."

He stood, still chuckling. "It's kinda nice to see karma coming around." He patted my shoulder. "I get to be PopPop and laugh. You get to be the heavy. Ah, life is good." He walked away, glancing over his shoulder. "Don't be too hard on them, Liam. They're kids. Find middle ground. I always did with you, and you turned out pretty damn good." He paused. "Maybe you need to turn them over to the master."

I mulled over his words, letting the boys tire themselves out in the water. They climbed out and headed my way. I waited until they sat down, wrapped in towels, rubbing their hair, looking pleased with themselves.

"How did you get out? Nothing alerted me."

AJ scoffed. "I bypassed that on Reid's program. Really, it was too easy."

Brock spoke up. "Too nice a night to stay in bed." He high-fived AJ. "And we beat Reid. Awesome night."

"Not so fast, young man," I said, letting some anger bleed into my voice.

"C'mon, Dad. It was just a swim."

"If something happened and you were alone, one or both of you could drown. How would you feel then? Think about your mother."

"We're advanced swimmers."

"What if there was an intruder? Found you here alone? What if they kidnapped you?"

They both had the nerve to laugh. "Dad, PopPop has this place locked down tight. We're perfectly safe here."

They were right and I was grasping at straws and I knew it, but I had to make them understand.

"Let me be clear. When I lock up the house, you are not allowed out of it again until I unlock it the next day. Do you understand?" I held up my hand before they could protest. "You want to go for a late swim? You ask. You want to roast marshmallows and sleep on the beach? You get permission." I paused. "Unless your behavior changes, all the computer stuff goes. Every bit of it. Nothing in your room, no workspace, nothing."

They looked shocked. "Dad—"

"Nope. I'm not listening. Now, back to the house and in bed. You're going somewhere in the morning with me." I pointed my finger. "Now."

I followed them, watching them walk ahead of me. I hated to pull the grounding thing and threatening the computer access, but that was the only way to get their attention.

And in the morning, I planned on getting backup to help.

The next morning, I frog-marched the boys over to Reid's. He was on his deck, a cup of coffee at his elbow and a laptop open in front of him. To this day, he always had one close.

"Ah, the troublemakers," he said with a smirk. "Your grandfather warned me I might see you this morning."

"Your disciples bypassed something on your program and escaped again," I said.

"Really?" he asked, incredulous. "What?"

AJ let out a string of words I didn't understand, but they impressed Reid.

"Interesting. I didn't think you could override that."

"I figured it out," AJ said smugly.

I pointed to the table. "Sit down."

Reid grinned. "Am I inheriting them?"

"The only thing that interests them is computers. You keep teaching them, so this is the deal. You get them twice a week. Teach them. Show them whatever you do. In return, I get their word they won't sneak out of the house, override my passwords, or anything else that I keep telling them to stop doing. No more changing their mother's cell phone ringtones to horror movie screams, making the doorbell ring when no one is there, or having the lights come on at three a.m. And no more adding porn to my laptop so it starts playing when I open it. No more tech pranks."

Reid glanced away, trying not to laugh.

I looked at AJ and Brock. It was like staring into my own face. The hair, their hazel eyes, even their stubborn jaws and the shape and size of their bodies. I could tell them apart because they were my sons, although on occasion, even I messed up. But Brock had a little scar over his left eyebrow from a tumble when he was three, so that was the best way to make sure. Right now, they looked uncertain and worried.

"You get time with Reid. Time with your computers. You are also going to help me on the grounds. You're going to stop the antics and the escaping. Or, as I told you last night—it all goes. No more computers, no more anything with Reid. You'll go to summer school."

They looked horrified. Nothing was worse to them than being in a classroom.

"It's your choice."

Reid nodded. "I agree with your dad. I love teaching you boys, but if you're only causing trouble with the stuff I show you, I'll stop."

They nodded in unison. "We'll do it."

Reid narrowed his eyes. "If you lie, I'll figure it out. You play me, it's done."

"No, we'll do it!" AJ said. "Promise."

"Yeah, Dad. We're sorry. We'll do better," Brock begged. "Honest. We just get bored."

Reid laughed under his breath. "Not anymore."

———

I returned to the house and headed to the kitchen. Paige and Lucy were at the table, drinking coffee. I poured a cup and sat down, rubbing my face.

Lucy grinned. "The boys with their new master?"

I had to chuckle. "Reid wanted to talk to them in private." I took a sip of the hot brew, enjoying the intense flavor. "He's been dying to spend more time with them. Now's his chance."

Paige smiled. "You were pretty stern."

Lucy grinned, her smile as wide and bright as it was the day I met her. "Still thrilled to have sons, Daddy?"

I had to laugh. They teased me about it all the time.

"I should have stopped at you girls," I admitted. "You were far easier."

Beth and Ronan had two children, Paul had two, and Jeremy had one. On days like today, they seemed the sensible group.

I looked at Paige. "Why'd we have so many kids anyway?"

She laughed as she stood to get more coffee. She stopped by my chair, leaning close. "I think your cock had a lot to do with it, Liam darling," she whispered in my ear.

"Hmm," I murmured, grabbing her and kissing her. "I think you were part of the problem. Always too damn sexy."

Lucy groaned. "Can the two of you *not*? *Please*?" she asked, but there was another smile on her face.

I let Paige go and focused on Lucy. She looked pretty and polished—grown-up. I still wasn't sure how that happened so quickly. She looked like Paige, although she was a little taller. She was sweet and funny and incredibly smart. I was very proud of her—we both were. She tucked a loose piece of hair behind her ear with her hand, her prosthesis now simply an extension of herself. She had come so far. She was studying to be a children's psychologist. She was going to be a great one.

"Summer classes today?"

She nodded. "I only have two, Daddy. I like school."

I loved the fact that she still called me Daddy, not Dad. All the girls did, but the boys preferred Dad. I also loved the fact that she chose to live at home while going to school.

She stood and dropped a kiss to my head. "I'll see you later. We're still doing movie night, even if the boys are in trouble, right?"

"Yeah, we are."

She passed Erin on the way out of the kitchen. My little bee hadn't changed much, except now she was a little taller but still tiny. She was the quiet one, she preferred plants to people, and me to everyone else.

Dressed in overalls, with her dark hair in pigtails, she was adorable as she bent and kissed my cheek. "I just need some breakfast, Daddy, then we can head out. I'm so excited to start!"

I chuckled at her enthusiasm.

Her future was set. The earth and flowers were what she loved the most, and there was no doubt who would be taking over Branching Outward one day. She knew more about plants and landscaping than I did. She had a hive of bees on the edge of the property and spent hours with her little namesakes. She kept everyone in delicious honey and beeswax candles that she loved to make with Paige.

Today, we were creating a new garden at Ava's. Erin had designed the entire thing, and we would begin the process this morning.

"Where's Shannon?" I asked. "I thought she said she wanted to help."

Erin chuckled. "She will—later. She's still sleeping." She met my eyes with a grin. "You know she's not a morning person."

Paige laughed as she sat beside me, sliding a plate of toasted bagels on the table. "If it were an Olympic sport, she'd get a gold medal."

She did love to sleep—always had. As she was still a teenager, it seemed to be her favorite thing. That and hanging with her friends on the beach. But she was a good kid, did well in school, and still loved to spend time with us once in a while. I was good with that.

None of the girls had ever given us any trouble.

Our sons made up for it.

Paige touched my face, bringing me back from my musings.

"The boys will be fine."

I smiled and captured her hand, holding it to my face. She always knew what I was thinking.

"Reid will keep them busy," I agreed. "Dad had given him a heads-up, and I think he had some plans."

She nodded. "I'm sure he does."

———————

Eight years later, I watched my boys walk across the stage and accept their diplomas. Tall, handsome, and broad, they stood head and shoulders above most of their classmates. They were easier to tell apart these days. AJ wore his hair longer and liked pants and polo shirts. Brock kept his hair short and was constantly in jeans and T-shirts.

They'd changed after a summer of Reid's tutelage. They were still a handful, but they were focused—at least as focused as nine-year-olds could be. The boys were still mischievous, and I was certain a lot of the pranks at school could be traced back to them, but they were better at not getting caught. They kept me on my toes, and I had to admit, they kept me laughing. Ronan got them into working out as well, which helped channel some of their restless energy.

They were planning on opening up their own company. No university for them. Reid was behind them, saying they had surpassed him in their expertise with computers. AJ could write programs that boggled my mind. Brock could build a computer that made my head spin with its capabilities. I could only imagine their future.

I slipped my arm around Paige and tucked her close. Beside her, our daughters watched their younger brothers with wide grins. My parents beamed with pleasure.

The boys had grown and matured, and I couldn't be prouder.

Brock and AJ stood tall, both wearing the same shit-eating grin as they looked over the crowd. The back of my neck tingled, recognizing those matching troublemaking expressions. I met my dad's gaze over the girls' heads, both of us knowing something was up. I noticed AJ slip his hand inside his robe, and then it happened.

Fireworks began in the open field behind us, the sudden booms startling everyone in the crowd. Everyone except the boys. They grinned and laughed, high-fiving each other, then disappearing behind the rest of the students. The crowd watched the short display, and even the principal smiled, although he tried to fight it. It was a cloudy day, even the weather cooperating to make the bright lights more visible.

My dad howled in amusement. The girls and Mom chuckled. Paige dropped her head, trying not to show her amusement.

I couldn't contain my laughter. One last prank.

That was my boys.

Thank you so much for reading LOVED BY LIAM. I appreciate all reviews. Make sure to drop me an email with a link or tag me on social media.

Do you enjoy audiobooks? Check out MY SAVING GRACE Vested Interest: ABC Corp Book #1 now available to listen.

If you have just started reading this series and would like to get to know the Liam's parents, start with the prequel: BAM- The Beginning

ABC CORP CONTINUES WITH...

AGE OF AVA

Vested Interest: ABC Corp #4

Ava Callaghan

A woman working in a male-dominated field.

Organized, strong, and tenacious.

That's how she has to be to succeed.

Hunter Owens

A loner.

He needs no one, has no ties, and his future is an unanswered question mark.

It's all he knows.

Until the day their lives intersect.

He sees the woman she hides from the world.

She nurtures the part of him he lost long ago.

But they both agree—their connection is temporary.

They are only for now.

Can their stubborn natures allow them to bend and accept that maybe, just maybe, there is more to life than they believed?

That love can heal.

That happiness can exist.

That *for now* can be forever.

ALSO AVAILABLE FROM MORELAND BOOKS

Titles published under M. Moreland

Insta-Spark Collection

It Started with a Kiss

Christmas Sugar

An Instant Connection

An Unexpected Gift

Harvest of Love (coming soon)

Titles published under Melanie Moreland

The Contract Series

The Contract (Contract #1)

The Baby Clause (Contract #2)

The Amendment (Contract #3)

Vested Interest Series

BAM - The Beginning (Prequel)

Bentley (Vested Interest #1)

Aiden (Vested Interest #2)

Maddox (Vested Interest #3)

Reid (Vested Interest #4)

Van (Vested Interest #5)

Halton (Vested Interest #6)

Sandy (Vested Interest #7)

Vested Interest Box Set (Books 1-3)

Vested Interest/ABC Crossover

A Merry Vested Wedding

ABC Corp Series

My Saving Grace (Vested Interest: ABC Corp #1)

Finding Ronan's Heart (Vested Interest: ABC Corp #2)

Loved By Liam (Vested Interest: ABC Corp #3)

Age of Ava (Vested Interest: ABC Corp #4)

Men of Hidden Justice (Coming Soon)

The Boss

Second-In-Command

Mission Cove

The Summer of Us

Standalones

Into the Storm

Beneath the Scars

Over the Fence

My Image of You (Republishing Soon)

Changing Roles

Happily Ever After Collection

Revved to the Maxx

Heart Strings

ACKNOWLEDGMENTS

Lisa—thank you for all the laughs. You are a joy to work with

and I'm grateful for your knowledge.

Beth, Trina, Melissa, Peggy, and Deb—thank you for your valuable input, your keen eyes, and encouragement. Your comments make the story better—always.

Thank you to Avery and Carol for the extra help. I appreciate it greatly.

Karen— Every time I think you cannot give me more, you surprise me.

I am lucky to have you. I am not giving you up. Evah.

Kim—thanks for keeping Karen in line.

I know it's a full time, thankless endeavor.

I bow to you.

My reader group, Melanie's Minions—love you all.

Melanie's Literary Mob—my promo team—you do me proud and I love our interactions.

Your support is amazing and humbling. Thank you for asking for this story.

To all the bloggers and readers. Thank you for everything you do. Shouting your love of books—of my work, posting, sharing—your recommendations keep my TBR list full, and the support you have shown me is deeply appreciated.

And my Matthew. I love you. Always.

ABOUT THE AUTHOR

NYT/WSJ/USAT international bestselling author Melanie Moreland, lives a happy and content life in a quiet area of Ontario with her beloved husband of thirty-plus years and their rescue cat, Amber. Nothing means more to her than her friends and family, and she cherishes every moment spent with them.

While seriously addicted to coffee, and highly challenged with all things computer-related and technical, she relishes baking, cooking, and trying new recipes for people to sample. She loves to throw dinner parties, and enjoys traveling, here and abroad, but finds coming home is always the best part of any trip.

Melanie loves stories, especially paired with a good wine, and enjoys skydiving (free falling over a fleck of dust) extreme snowboarding (falling down stairs) and piloting her own helicopter (tripping over her own feet.) She's learned happily ever afters, even bumpy ones, are all in how you tell the story.

Melanie is represented by Flavia Viotti at Bookcase Literary Agency. For any questions regarding subsidiary or translation rights please contact her at flavia@bookcaseagency.com

Connect with Melanie

Like reader groups? Lots of fun and giveaways! Check it out Melanie Moreland's Minions

Join my newsletter for up-to-date news, sales, book announcements and excerpts (no spam). Click here to sign up Melanie Moreland's newsletter

or visit https://bit.ly/MMorelandNewsletter

Visit my website www.melaniemoreland.com

facebook.com/authormoreland

twitter.com/morelandmelanie

instagram.com/morelandmelanie

Made in the USA
Monee, IL
31 July 2021